TWIST IN THE TALE

SHORT STORIES

VOLUME 2

A J BOOTHMAN

ALVASDA KEREZARD

TWIST IN THE TALE SHORT STORIES

Published by Alvasda Kerezard 2023

ISBN 978-1-916537-02-6

TWIST IN THE TALE
SHORT STORIES

TWIST IN THE TALE SHORT STORIES

SPIDER

TWIST IN THE TALE SHORT STORIES

"Can anyone tell me the most poisonous spider species in the world?"

The small, squat man stood behind the podium and observed the sparsely filled lecture theatre. There had been more at the start but gradually the room had thinned out. He could see the boredom etched on the faces of the meagre group remaining, spread out across the auditorium. One young man was draped across the desk with his head buried in his crossed arms. He did not like giving talks, he had told the Head of Entomology that, but all to no avail. Everyone insisted that following his prize he was expected to do it. So, here he was, Norman Whitlaw, giving his mandatory lecture. He ran his hand over the few strands of hair that attempted to cover his balding head. The young man raised his head wearily.

"The Funnel-web Spider," he mumbled before slumping back down.

"Atrax robustus," replied Norman, relieved to get a response. "Certainly, it has been responsible for several deaths in Australia, but not the most venomous I am afraid."

He scanned the room hoping to elicit another guess.

"The Black Widow Spider?" suggested a young woman timidly in a quiet voice.

"Ah, Latrodectus mactans, you are getting warmer."

Norman smiled at her in eager anticipation. She adjusted her spectacles and lowered her head. He was aware of the silence becoming uncomfortable as he took out his handkerchief and wiped the beads of sweat from his forehead. He reached down behind the podium and placed a small glass box on top.

7

"It's this," he announced proudly. "The Whitlaw Widow."

Inside the box a small black spider with its legs extended over twice the length of its body clung to the front glass wall, exposing its green underside to the assembly, who suddenly became more alert. Even the young man slouched over the desk raised his head with eyes wide open.

"This is Nancy, a member of the Latrodectus species which includes the black widow spider, brown widow spider and red widow spider. It is exceedingly rare, inhabiting only a handful of the West Indian Islands. I discovered Nancy in Monserrat. As you can see she very closely resembles the black widow spider. About the same size and colour with a one-inch shiny black body. In fact, the only visual distinction between a black widow and Whitlaw widow is that the abdomen is dark green as opposed to red. The male is smaller and even rarer because, as with all widow spiders, the female kills and eats him after mating."

Norman was distracted by the sudden opening of a side door beside him. He turned his head and became transfixed by the vison of beauty gliding into the theatre, her long, golden hair cascading around her angelic face. A short black dress hugged her hourglass figure and a burgundy handbag hanging from her shoulder swayed as she ascended a couple of steps and sat in the front row directly in front of him. He was mesmerised by her sparkling eyes and ruby red lips.

"Sorry I'm late," she said in a sweet, honeyed voice. "Please continue."

"Um, yes, where was I?" he flustered. "Nancy, yes Nancy. Well, I call her Nancy after Anansi, the Akan folklore character famous throughout Africa and the Caribbean who took the form

8

of a spider. Nancy is twice as venomous as a brown widow and four times that of a black. One bite and you would be dead within seconds, there is no known antidote. So, you can see, Nancy is certainly not a nancy."

He paused expectantly for laughter, but none was forthcoming.

"Yes, well," he mumbled uncomfortably shuffling from foot to foot. "That concludes my talk, if anyone would like a closer look at Nancy they are welcome."

He watched as everyone filed towards the exits. Disappointedly he removed his worn jacket from the chair behind and slipped it on. No-one seemed to see the beauty of Nancy like he did, he thought, shaking his head sadly. He turned back to the podium, his spirits suddenly lifted, stooped, peering into the glass cabinet stood the woman with the long, golden hair.

"So, this is the famous Whitlaw widow," she mused.

"Um, yes."

"I saw you on TV last week getting your prize and just had to come and meet you. £100,000 wasn't it?"

"Um, yes, for research."

"Sonya Preston, "she announced standing up and extending her bejewelled hand.

Norman took her hand feeling its velvety softness and captivated by her perfectly manicured, scarlet fingernails. The golden bracelets around her wrist jangled as they shook.

"It's Norman isn't it?"

"Yes, that's right."

"And you're some sort of ologist?"

"An arachnologist."

"Simply fascinating. Where do you keep your spiders?"

"Most are kept in my university lab but I have a small private collection at home."

"Doesn't your wife mind?"

"I'm not married."

"Well, your girlfriend?"

"I don't have a girlfriend," he replied quietly lowering his head.

"A rich, handsome and successful man like you must be fighting the ladies off."

"Not really," he mumbled staring at his shoes. "I'm not particularly successful or rich. I wouldn't say handsome either, no woman has ever said so."

"Well, I think you are."

Norman looked meekly up at her beautiful face, who was this goddess who thought he was handsome?

"I'd love to see your collection, "she gushed.

"I can show you around the lab."

"I meant your private collection."

"You want to come to my house?"

"Oh, yes, I'd love to."

A look of uncertainty came over Norman's face, no woman had asked to come to his house before, in fact, no woman had been in his house before, at least not a guest. He looked up at her big, beautiful eyes and coy smile. She reached into her handbag and removed her lipstick. Norman watched her every move as she took off the lid and turned the bottom. The bright ruby stick emerged slowly. She looked into Norman's eyes as she sensually glided the tip over her luscious lips, back and forth until her full lips shone bright red.

"I'm free this evening," she said boldly replacing the lipstick into her bag.

"I'm not sure."

"Do you have something else on?"

"Well, no."

"It's settled then, shall we say eight?"

This was unbelievable, an attractive woman wanted to come to his house. His mouth was dry and he could feel beads of sweat beginning to form on his forehead again.

"Eight will be fine."

"Until eight then'" she said striding towards the exit.

"What about my address? he called.

"That's ok, I have it already."

****

Norman scrutinised his appearance worriedly in the mirror, his shirt still looked a bit crumpled despite his best efforts to iron it. He shoved the bottom into his trousers in a vain attempt to stretch out the wrinkles. This was a momentous occasion, he had never had a guest in his house before, especially not one so glamorous. He adjusted his tie and combed the few strands of hair across his head. The doorbell rang. He took one last look at his reflection and scurried down the stairs.

"What a lovely home," remarked Sonya as he opened the door.

She walked elegantly into the hall, her long black dress swaying as she moved, the high slit exposing her shapely legs and stocking top. Her full golden hair seemed even more radiant than this morning and her red lips fuller and more alluring. He was bewitched by this exquisite muse. She swivelled on her high heeled shoes to face him making him look down embarrassed by his own thoughts. On her feet were dainty, pink, stiletto shoes with little bows on the heels.

"I-I like your pink shoes," he mumbled.

"Fuchsia."

"Pardon?"

"They are fuchsia, not pink, designed by Christian Louboutin."

"Oh."

She opened the flap of her handbag and applied lipstick. Norman watched as she ran the tip over her luscious ruby red lips. She put it back in her bag and closed the flap. He studied

12

the bag, he was sure it was the same one she had earlier, burgundy with gold trim. Sonya noticed him staring at it.

"It's Cartier, real calfskin with a lambskin interior, wonderfully soft and smooth," she exuded, gently running her hand delicately over it. "So luxurious."

Norman led her into the small sitting room. She sat down on the old, worn sofa and looked around the sparsely furnished room. Thin, grey curtains hung limply across the window and an old-fashioned faded floral carpet covered the floor. A cheap-looking small table and single wooden chair sat in the corner.

"C-can I get you a drink, I don't have much, I think there is a bottle of wine somewhere."

"Maybe later, come and sit beside me," she said patting the seat beside her. "I want to know all about you."

Norman trundled to the sofa and perched uncomfortably on the edge, wringing his small, stubby hands together and staring down.

"Not much to tell, really."

"So, you are not married?"

"No."

"Have you ever been?"

"No."

"You do like women?"

"Oh, yes."

"I know, you just never met the right one. I always meet the wrong man."

"A-are you married then?"

"Not at present, but I have been, they're both dead now. Widowed twice and not even forty."

"I'm sorry."

"Who would think two rich, successful men would both succumb to accidents."

"H-how did they die?"

"The first drowned in a boating accident ten years ago, just fell overboard."

"Why didn't he swim back and climb back in?"

"He couldn't swim. Can you swim?

"Oh, yes, I learnt in school. What happened to the second?"

"Died in a car crash, brakes failed, do you have a car?"

"No, I can't drive, I go on the bus to the university."

"You carry spiders on the bus?"

"It's quite safe, they are always in their boxes, although I do have to cover them with a cloth as once a young female got quite hysterical upon seeing Nancy and I had to get off and walk home."

"That's terrible, "said Sonya soothingly placing her hand on his thigh.

Norman blushed as her soft hand gently stroked his leg.

"W-would you like to see my collection," he stammered.

Sonya smiled teasingly as she slowly lifted her hand.

"Certainly."

She followed Norman out of the room. In the hall he opened a side door and led her down a narrow staircase into the basement. As she walked down into the dimly lit basement she could feel the increasing heat.

"Nearly all the arachnids down here come from tropical climates so they must be kept warm," informed Norman.

In the centre of the basement was a wooden table and along each wall were shelves filled with glass cabinets of varying sizes. Sonya walked slowly around the room looking at the rows of spiders. She stopped at a cabinet containing several small, brown, hairy spiders with stout long legs.

"Wolf spiders," advised Norman. "Members of the Lyosidae family. I collected these in North America."

"What a wonderful collection."

"I'm glad you like it, most women go hysterical at the sight of the smallest spider."

"I'm not at all squeamish."

"On this shelf are all my widow spiders: black, red, brown, redback."

Sonya stood beside him and observed the different coloured spiders before turning to the table. In the centre she recognised Nancy in her small glass box.

"Ah, here's the discovery that won you all that lovely money."

"For research, "he said hastily.

She looked at his crumpled shirt and cheap trousers.

"I think you should spend some of the money on yourself. Maybe some new clothes, you want to look your best for your presentations. I think you would look very dashing in an Armani suit," she said batting her long eye-lashes.

"I don't really have a need for a suit, I mainly just work in my lab."

"What about when you go out?"

"I don't really go out, I spend most evenings in the basement," he said bashfully.

Sonya surveyed the table, it was bare except for a microscope and a rack containing a single, small, glass vial of white liquid.

"What's this?" she asked picking up the vial.

Norman quickly gripped her hand and kept the vial steady.

"It's poison."

He cautiously removed the vial from between her fingers.

"I extracted it from Nancy, one drop would kill you in seconds."

"You are so caring Norman," she purred caressing his arm.

16

"Yes, well, I wouldn't want anything to happen to you," he said weakly placing the vial back in the rack.

"You're so sweet, Norman. Let's go back upstairs and you can open that bottle of wine."

Sonya went back into the sitting room. The house was nice and big but could do with sprucing up she thought looking around, a new sofa, new curtains, new carpet. Norman entered carrying a glass of wine in one hand and a glass of milk in the other. He handed the wine to Sonya and sipped the milk.

"Aren't you having wine?"

"No, I don't drink."

"Never?"

"No, the wine was a present, it must have been in the cupboard for two years or more."

Sonya lifted the wine to her ruby lips, surprisingly good, she thought taking a big gulp.

"I love wine and fine dining, we should go to that new restaurant in the High Street."

"L-like a date? "spluttered Norman almost spilling the milk.

Sonya lifted the glass and drank the last of the wine.

"Yes, certainly," she smiled seductively.

That was how it all started, Norman Whitlaw had his very first date. That led to a second and a third, a whirlwind romance and within a month he was married. His life had changed

17

seemingly over night. Sonya moved into his house and immediately set about redecorating. She transformed the sitting room installing a cream, leather corner sofa and rosewood coffee table, replacing the drab grey curtains with plush velvet and the worn carpet with an oak wooden floor and Persian rug. He had spent more in a month than the previous five years but it was all worth it for Sonya.

Sonya lay sprawled out on the sofa, eyes closed, with a glass of wine in her hand and a near empty bottle on the coffee table beside her. She listened to the key being turned and the front door opening and closing. Plodding steps came down the hall and into the kitchen. She could hear the fridge door opening and the glug of pouring. More lumbering clumps in the hall and Norman entered the room, milk in hand.

"You're late today," she said without looking up.

"I had a meeting with the Head of Entomology about financing for the research trip to the Virgin Islands."

"When are you going?"

"I'm not, he said I had to finance it with the prize money."

"So, finance it with the prize money."

"There's hardly any left," he muttered looking around at the new luxury refurbishments.

Sonya emptied the wine into her mouth.

"Did you get your life insurance sorted out?"

"No, I didn't have time."

"You don't want to leave me penniless if something happens to you, do you?" she glowered turning her head and staring at him.

"No, of course not, I'll do it."

"Good, the forms are in my bag. You can fill them in now."

"Yes, dear," said Norman wearily.

Norman opened her Cartier bag, removed the forms and dutifully filled them in while Sonya re-filled her glass.

"I saw the most exquisite necklace In Tiffany's this morning," she said. "A pear-shaped diamond pendent designed by Elsa Peretti."

"How much was it?"

"£755."

"That's quite a lot, dear. I don't know if we can afford it."

"That's what my other husbands said," she replied coldly. "Leave the forms in my bag when you have finished and I'll post them tomorrow. I'm going up to bed."

She got up unsteadily, took her glass and teetered across the room and out. Norman surveyed the room, new sofa, new curtains and now she wanted a £755 necklace. He was conscious of all the money going out and he still had to finance his trip to the Virgin Islands. Perhaps this necklace would be the last thing he convinced himself. He returned to the forms.

Early Saturday morning Norman sat on the bus, he had told Sonya he was going to the university but he was not. He had checked his bank account and decided to do it. The bus stopped and he got off. The High Street was quite quiet as he walked past all the shops. He crossed into the pedestrian precinct and stood before the glass fronted shop looking apprehensively up at the lettering above, "Tiffany & Co." Inside the store he was greeted by an elegant, young woman.

"Welcome to Tiffany and Co., I'm Natalie" she beamed radiantly through pearly white teeth. "What can I show you today."

"I was interested in a diamond necklace," he replied fumbling in his jacket pocket. "I have the details here somewhere, I wrote them down. Here it is, a pear-shaped diamond necklace by Elsa Peretti, £755"

"Ah, yes, please come this way."

Norman followed her to a glass cabinet displaying necklaces of gold and silver with pendants of ruby and sapphire. She removed a necklace and placed it on the glass top. The light above glinted off the diamond making it shine with a light blue hue.

"A beautiful example of the art of Elsa Peretti," she gushed. "The diamond is .07 carat weight. The chain is sterling silver but you can change it to gold if you wish. We have some beautiful chains starting at £500."

"Just as it is, thank you."

Sonya looked around the basement at all the glass cabinets, they would all have to go. She didn't really care if the university took them or not, she could just as easily stamp on them one by one with her shoe. Norman's life insurance was finalised, it was time to act. In the glass box on the table Nancy had climbed the side wall to the top, almost as if she was watching as Sonya moved around scanning the room. Suddenly she stopped by a filing cabinet, on top was the vial rack with the solitary tube containing the spider venom. Carefully she lifted it and studied the white liquid inside. An idea suddenly filled her head, white, perfect. Upstairs she heard the key turning in the front door, Norman! What was he doing back so soon? She concealed the vial in her hand and hurried up the stairs. Outside Norman paused, holding the jewellery box, it was important Sonya didn't see it, it would spoil the surprise. He slipped it under his coat. Sonya reached the hall closing the door behind her just as the front door opened.

"Sonya!" he gasped.

"What are you doing home?" she blurted placing her hands behind her back.

"Um, well, I finished early. What have you been doing/"

"Nothing."

They stood in an awkward silence looking at each other.

"I-I'm just going to check on Nancy," he spluttered moving tentatively forwards.

"Ok," replied Sonya stepping slowly back.

Norman opened the basement door and walked down as casually as he could. Sonya watched him then turned and rushed into the kitchen. She frantically searched for a hiding place for the vial. She needed somewhere Norman would not find it. He was always looking for things he had misplaced. She

21

needed a place he never went. Fervently she scrutinised the kitchen. Where, oh, where? Maybe a glass of wine would calm her and help her think better. That's it, the wine rack. She knelt down and removed a bottle from the bottom, sliding the vial to the back and replacing it.

In the basement Norman took the box from under his coat. He opened the filing cabinet and placed it inside. This would be a nice surprise and make Sonya so happy, he thought, as he closed the drawer. He would give it to her this evening after dinner.

Norman looked through the window into the darkness before closing the curtains. Sonya watched his every move from the sofa as she sipped her wine. He observed her bag on the floor as he moved back and gradually lowered himself into the armchair pressing his fingertips together and studying her closely. She seemed anxious as she gingerly lifted the glass to her lips and took small, rapid sips. Did she know about the necklace? Had she guessed? Was he acting too suspiciously? He lowered his hands and sat on them. Sonya emptied her glass.

"I think, I'll open another bottle," she said determinedly getting up. "Do you want a glass of milk?"

"Oh, yes, thank you, dear."

Norman watched her disappear and hurried to her bag, picking it up swiftly and going to the door. He stuck his head out into the hall and listened. In the kitchen he could hear Sonya moving about, the fridge door opening and the glugging of milk being poured. He rushed into the hall and down into the basement.

Sonya retracted the bottle of wine from the bottom of the rack, reached to the back and lifted the vial. She moved slowly and held the poison over the glass. Cautiously she tipped the vial. The poison flowed into the milk. She took a spoon from the drawer and stirred it, there was no discoloration. Carefully she washed the spoon and replaced it in the drawer. There must be no trace of the venom. She lifted the glass and sniffed it, no odour, perfect.

In the basement, Norman took the necklace out of its box. He studied the diamond, it was indeed a very beautiful jewel, Sonya would be so happy. He opened the flap of her bag and slipped the jewellery inside. Closing it he placed it on the floor under the table just as Sonya entered carrying the milk.

"I thought I heard you come down here," she said.

"Um, yes, I won't be long, dear."

"Take all the time in the world."

She placed the milk on the table carefully before walking slowly and decisively away, stopping at the bottom of the stairs, turning her head and smiling knowingly.

She disappeared, did she know, he wondered. He wanted it to be a surprise. He lifted the glass to his lips and stopped. Before him in the glass box nancy was racing around crazily. He remained still watching as she ran around the walls and ceiling, he had never seen her acting so strangely. He put the glass down and looked around the room, everything seemed normal. The other spiders were as dormant as usual. He shrugged his shoulders, lifted the glass and drank. Suddenly, Nancy stopped moving, she remained statuesque on the box ceiling. For an instant everything became still and silent. Then Norman lurched forwards onto the table grabbing his chest, gasping for breath, his eyes bulging. Desperately, he tried to call out but it was just a weak groan. He could feel his body going into paralysis, he looked feverishly about him, the glass cabinets going in and out of focus as his vision blurred. Then he saw it, the empty vial rack. His mind raced with the horrific realisation. With his remaining strength he knocked the glass box off the table. It crashed to the ground and shattered. Norman staggered to his feet, smiled weakly and collapsed with a heavy thud.

Sonya descended the stairs into the basement. A cruel smile spread across her lips as she looked at Norman's lifeless body. Under the table she spotted her bag. She bent down and picked it up. As it raised shards of glass fell from it. She opened the flap, removed the lipstick and lifted it up to her face. Immediately her expression turned to horror. On the back of her hand sat Nancy. For a moment they seemed transfixed, looking at each other, then she felt the sharp prick. She fell backwards her body convulsing as the poison spread quickly. Her senses began to numb. As she took her last, weak gasps she watched Nancy scurrying across the floor and disappearing below the floorboards.

KITTY

AUTHOR'S INTRODUCTION

Everyone has heard of the famous dog show, Crufts, but did you know there is an equivalent competition for cats, the Supreme Cat Show? There are categories for adult cats and kittens and honours for different breeds, leading to the ultimate accolade of Supreme Champion. For cat enthusiasts this is the greatest prize of them all and they will go to extreme lengths to win this coveted award.

In this tale Alice is a delivery rider struggling to make ends meet until she meets a strange, old woman obsessed with her cat. She sees an opportunity to improve her life, but will things go as planned?

Alice cycled past the deserted building site, the cars roared on the flyover above. She entered the parking lot and placed her bike against one of the multitude of porta cabins. On the steel wall she read the sign, The Frying Dutch Pan. The name always made her smile, even now as she felt the rain begin to fall. She pulled the hood of her anorak over her head and looked up at the darkening sky, sighing wearily, another gloomy evening. Around her the other porta cabins displayed their names: Barry's Burgers, The Pizza Place, Paradiso Italiano. She stared at the last one, Paradiso Italiano, a customer would be forgiven for thinking their food was being prepared by a gourmet chef in a Michelin star restaurant as opposed to a teenager, fresh out of catering college, cooking in a small, windowless porta cabin in a car park. A scooter pulled up beside her, the rider dismounting and racing to the door of Paradiso Italiano, the engine still running. It was opened by a pimply youth in a white jacket who handed him two small cardboard boxes. He quickly placed them into his backpack, got back on the scooter and sped away, no doubt to deliver tonight's haute cuisine to some unsuspecting punter.

She knocked on the door of The Frying Dutch Pan.

"Alice, come in, almost ready," said a young man opening it.

Alice was hit by the greasy aroma as she stepped inside. She looked around the small, dingy space, the phrase "couldn't swing a cat in it," springing to mind. The deep fat fryer bubbled away furiously while burgers and sausages sizzled on the griddle. She noted the bin overflowing with supermarket food packages and shook her head.

"People could make this themselves, Jack"

27

"Are you trying to run me out of a job?" he replied as he flipped the burgers.

"No, I'm just saying."

"I have to admit, I did hope for something a bit better than working in a "Dark Kitchen" when I left college. Still, a job 's a job."

Alice knew that all too well. In June she had graduated from university with the world at her feet. She dreamt of working in television or radio, making life changing documentaries or writing in depth articles for national newspapers and magazines. Four months later, here she was delivering fatty slop on a rickety bike in the rain, so much for a degree in Media Studies.

Still, she hadn't given up hope, if she could save enough money she could make her own programmes. Buy a good quality camera and set up her own channel on YouTube and Patreon and Tik Tok and every other media platform. Then the BBC would give her a job. Or maybe she would be making enough money to be an independent documentary maker.

"Alice!"

She snapped out of her delicious fantasy.

"I've been calling you for ages," said Jack holding up a small plastic bag and waving it in front of her face. "What were you so deep in thought about?"

"Nothing, "she replied quickly, taking the bag and opening her back pack.

"It's for a Mrs. Willett, Kitty Cottage, Oak Tree Lane."

"I don't think I've been there before."

"No, Terry Reilly used to take the deliveries. Don't get talking about her cat for God's sake, you'll be there all night."

"I haven't seen Terry for weeks."

"He stopped coming, just disappeared one night. That's the way it is in the delivery game, when people have had enough they just leave."

"Might have got a proper job," said Alice strapping on the large square back pack and heading for the door.

"Careful that doesn't tip you over the back of the bike," called Jack laughing at the big, orange box dwarfing her small body.

She got on the saddle and started pedalling. Oh great, she thought, feeling the rain fall heavier. It wasn't surprising Terry had left, who in their right mind would want to do this for a living. She reminded herself that it was only temporary and that one day she would be a rich and famous documentary maker. Her spirits began to lift as she rode away from the gloom of the town and the road became quieter. The houses and buildings began to thin out and soon she was surrounded by fields. She turned into a narrow lane surrounded by tall oak trees on either side. It was very picturesque despite the increasing darkness, open fields and isolated cottages behind magnificent trees and hedges. She rounded a bend feeling icy water splash up her socks as the bike went through a small puddle. Up ahead a dim lamp illuminated a little, chocolate box cottage, a thin plume of smoke drifting from the chimney. Alice stopped at the gate and looked at the thatched roof and tiny windows. She dismounted, the iron gate creaked as she pushed it open and wheeled the bike along the narrow path that dissected the overgrown garden. The rain beat down upon her anorak and she hurried to the old wooden door. She leant the bike against the wall, took off the back pack and pulled the zip. It moved about two inches then stopped dead. That's all I need, she thought, tugging at it while the constant rain began to penetrate her jacket. She put it down on the wet ground and yanked the zip furiously, becoming increasingly agitated. Suddenly the door opened.

"Come in, dearie, you'll catch your death of cold out there."

Alice looked up at the little, hunched,, old lady with grey hair stood in the doorway dressed in an old, grey cardigan and plaid skirt.

"I'm ok, thanks, The Frying Dutch Pan, meal delivery," she announced tugging the zip with all her might. "I'll have it in a minute, its stuck."

She gave the zip a massive jerk and flew backwards, landing on the soaking grass with the metal pull in her hand.

"Come on now, we can open it inside," insisted the old woman kindly stooping over and picking up the back pack. "You can have a nice cup of tea."

Alice got up running her had along the drenched back of her trousers, she was about to protest but the old woman had already disappeared into the cottage. A cup of hot tea would be nice, she thought, and it might give a chance for the rain to ease off. She entered a narrow, dimly lit hallway. At the end she could see into the kitchen, the old woman stood at the sink filling an old brass kettle from the tap.

"Go into the sitting room, dearie, and warm yourself by the fire," she said gesturing to a door on the right.

Alice opened it and immediately felt the heat. A fire roared, the flames dancing up the brick chimney. She approached gratefully and extended her arms, the warmth drying her cold, wet hands. The mantel piece was full of ornaments, all cats of different colours, some sitting, some lying. She picked up a white porcelain cat, surprised at its weight. It was beautifully detailed with whiskers and a small button nose, it seemed to be quite old, she wondered if it was valuable. She replaced it, turned with her back to the fire and surveyed the room. An old, wooden rocking chair sat in the corner. She moved across and gently pushed it, listening to it softly creaking as it swayed back and forth. On the floor was a large rug with a burgundy, medallion centre and beige border, on which sat a mahogany, antique chest. Beside it was a rather worn sofa, partially covered by a red throw and embroidered, gold-coloured, floral cushions. On the wall behind it hung a large painting of a white cat sitting on a purple, velvet cushion. Its fur seemed to shine as it held its head up, almost regal in its appearance. She moved around the room to the tall glass fronted cabinet against the adjacent wall. The inside was full of trophies and plaques. She read the engravings:

HOME COUNTIES CAT SOCIETY

CHAMPION 2019

KITTY

CAMBRIDESHIRE CAT CLUB

CHAMPION 2020

KITTY

KENT & SURREY CAT ASSOCIATION

CHAMPION 2021

KITTY

Others were from competitions in Oxfordshire, Sussex and even as far north as Blackpool. Pinned to the wood behind were rosettes from Essex, Berkshire, Hampshire and all the neighbouring counties spanning the last three years, all with the same name, Kitty. On the centre of the middle shelf was an empty plinth with a photo of a white cat behind. Alice moved her face up to the glass and examined the photo, it was the identical cat as in the painting. She turned around and almost fell back against the cabinet with fright. Sat on the sofa, staring up at her with big, copper-coloured eyes was the very same cat, Kitty.

Alice's heart melted as she looked at her cute, snub nose and chubby cheeks. She approached and stroked her hand along her snowy, white fur, so rich and soft. The cat purred lightly as she caressed behind her small, rounded ears.

"Here you are, a nice hot cup of tea."

The old woman entered carrying a silver tray containing an ornamental ceramic tea pot, with matching milk jug and sugar bowl and two dinky cups. She placed it on top of the chest.

"I see you've met Kitty, she likes you, I can tell."

"She is very beautiful, what type of cat is she?"

"A Persian White, do you take milk or sugar, dearie?"

"Just milk, please. "Her fur is as soft as silk."

"It's her special diet that makes it so smooth and sleek."

"What's her special diet?"

"Liver and kidney, here you are, dear."

Alice took the cup and sat down beside Kitty. The handle was so dinky she had to use the tips of her fingers to lift it off the saucer. She raised it carefully to her lips and felt the tea warm her inside as she took a sip.

"I was admiring all the trophies and rosettes she has won."

"She's won all the competitions she has entered, dear, all bar one."

The old woman sat on the other side of Kitty and looked into the cabinet at the empty plinth. Alice followed her gaze.

"What competition is that?"

"The Supreme Cat Show Supreme Champion, the greatest prize in the country." replied the old woman yearningly

"Is that like Crufts?"

"It's better than Crufts, it's for cats."

33

A determined look came over her face.

"This will be our year, won't it, Kitty?"

The cat's ears pricked up.

Alice looked at her watch and put the cup back on the tray.

"It's time I was getting back."

"Are you sure you don't want another cup, dearie?"

"No, thank you," she said standing up.

Kitty moved slowly across the sofa and climbed onto the old woman's lap. She ran her hand along it's creamy fur, sipping her tea and staring at the cabinet, seemingly oblivious to Alice waiting patiently.

"It's £12 for the food," she prompted.

"Ah, of course, I had quite forgotten. Can you lift up the tray, dearie?"

Alice picked up the tray. The old woman bent forward and opened the chest. Alice could not believe her eyes, it was full of notes, fivers, tens, twenties, even a few bundles of fifties. How much was in here, thousands, tens of thousands?

"I don't trust banks, dear," said the old woman noting the astonishment on her face.

"Aren't you afraid of being burgled?"

"No, it's very safe here, I don't even lock the front door."

She pulled out a £10 note and delved to the bottom fishing out a handful of coins.

"Here you are," she said placing the £10 note and two one-pound coins on the tray. "And something for yourself."

Alice looked at the faded 20 pence piece.

She rode home, the rain turning to a miserable drizzle. Unbelievable, she thought, 20p, she had cycled all that way in the pouring rain for 20p. It wasn't as though the old woman couldn't afford it, there must have been £50,000 in that chest, maybe more.

Thirty minutes later she was back in her small flat, looking up ruefully at the damp patch spreading out from the corner of the bedroom ceiling as she removed her wet clothes and slipped into her pyjamas. She went into the kitchen and removed the last of the bread from an almost bare cupboard before opening the fridge door to reveal a couple of yogurt cartons, a mouldy piece of cheese and half a tin of baked beans. Kitty was probably having salmon and caviar and she was on beans on toast again, she thought, picking up the tin. Her mind went back to the chest of money as she heated the beans on the hob and put the bread into the toaster. How had the old woman gotten all that cash? There must have been tens of thousands, maybe even a hundred thousand pounds. She stirred the beans around the pot as they began to bubble, she had seen a number of fifty-pound note bundles scattered randomly around the rest of the notes, the old woman probably didn't even know how much there was. An idea suddenly sprung into her head as she put the toast on a plate and piled the beans on top. She put the plate on a tray and went into the sitting room. The old woman would probably not miss a few bundles. She sat on the sagging sofa and began to eat. The front door was never locked, it would be easy. Maybe just take two bundles of fifties, all she needed was a couple of thousand pounds. She was being ridiculous, she wasn't a thief, what if she got caught, she would lose her job, wind up with a criminal record, perhaps even have to serve time in prison. No, best to put the notion out of her mind. She finished eating and returned the tray to the kitchen, on the counter beside her keys she saw the twenty pence piece. Twenty pence? The old woman was certainly miserly, probably how she had amassed all that money, probably deserved to be robbed, it would be like stealing from Scrooge. She would be a modern-day Robin Hood, stealing from the rich to give to, well, herself. Think of all the good she could do with the money, making documentaries that would change the world, certainly not blowing it all on, when all is said and done, a moggy. It would need to be done at night when it was dark and no-one was around. Being a delivery cyclist would give her the perfect reason to be in the lane. She could pull her hood up over her head and wrap a scarf around her face. Her cycling gloves would ensure no fingerprints were left at the scene. She went into the bedroom and climbed into bed, this could actually work.

The following day she was back on her bike riding around the streets, all foolish thoughts of burglary dismissed from her mind. The air was cold and the sky cloudy as she cycled from kitchens and restaurants to houses and flats over and over again. Was this forever to be her life?

She returned home mid-afternoon to find an ominous brown envelope on the floor. With some trepidation she opened it, her gas and electricity bill, final reminder. She placed it down and leant resignedly on the kitchen counter, burying her face in her arms, how long could she go on living like this. Out of the corner of her eye she saw the twenty pence piece beside her. Slowly she extended her hand and picked it up. She stood up and stared at it decisively, she would do it.

It was dark when Alice rode into the lane, thick cloud covered the sky. She stopped a little way from the cottage, dismounted, pushed the bike between the trees and laid it down, concealed behind a large oak. Her head was covered by her hood and a scarf was wrapped around her face so only her eyes were visible. She peered nervously up and down the quiet, deserted lane. Tentatively she made her way towards the cottage. Her heart was beating faster as she approached the little house and she tightened her grip on the small torch in her gloved hand. She looked up at the street lamp, the bulb was even dimmer than yesterday, barely providing any illumination, little more than a yellow glow. Maybe the gods were on her side, she thought, as she eased the gate open and moved stealthily down the garden path. She stopped at the front door and lightly turned the handle. Her breathing accelerated, the door opened slowly and quietly. She looked into the dark hallway and stepped inside. Her emotions heightened with a mixture of terror and excitement. She walked down the hall through the blackness, not yet daring to turn on the torch. One slow, deliberate step after the other until she stood facing the siting room door. She lowered her shaking hand onto the knob and turned it. Gradually she opened the door, stepped inside and softly closed it behind her. In the grate the embers smouldered with an orange hue. So far so good, she thought, switching on the torch. She shone the beam around the room, the cabinet filled with trophies, the old rocking chair, still and silent, the sofa covered in cushions and finally onto the wooden chest. Quickly she knelt down before it. She placed the torch on the ground and placing both hands on the lid began to prise it open. Alice was surprised at its weight but lifted it steadily until it rested back on its hinges. She retrieved the torch and shone it inside. Her eyes widened as she looked at the mountain of notes, running her hand over the top, she had never seen so much money in all her life. Suddenly, she heard a creak that stopped her breathing and sent her heart beating through her chest. She whirled around and shone the beam in the direction of the sound. The old rocking chair was gently swaying back and forth with a constant, haunting creaking. On the seat two large copper-coloured eyes observed her every action, Kitty. Alice let a huge sigh of relief, she must have been in the room all the time and just leapt onto the chair. The rocking chair slowed and stopped. Alice returned to the chest, just take the money and get out of here, she thought, then slumped onto the floor. She lay still, blood seeping onto the rug from a gaping wound in the back of her head. The light went on, the old woman stood with a hammer in her hand. Over her cardigan she wore a white apron, splattered with blood. She put the hammer down and produced a large carving knife. Kitty looked at the gleaming silver blade and jumped onto the rug, licking her lips.

"I was getting worried, Kitty," said the old woman kneeling beside the body and hovering the knife above. "We had almost run out of your special food. Do you want liver or kidney tonight?"

VOODOO

The white van was parked on the gravel court in front of the large, grandiose house. Snowflakes gently fluttered in the breeze, landing on the ground and dissolving into nothingness as the sun began to set. Inside the spacious entrance hall Akande perched on the top of a step ladder carefully painting the cornice above the door. He was tall and slim, moving the brush gracefully, his dark skin contrasting against his white overalls. Around his neck he wore a bead necklace adorned with charms and amulets. He descended and looked up at his work, smiling with satisfaction. Placing the brush down he approached the adjacent oak door and knocked.

"Come!" boomed a deep voice.

Akande turned the handle and entered. Immediately he was hit by the heat blazing from the fireplace. Against the opposing wall stood a large wooden bookshelf filled with rows of old, leather-bound books. At the back of the room Cornelius Kenworthy sat behind an impressive mahogany desk, his head bowed studying the papers before him illuminated by the reading lamp. Akande waited patiently, observing the old man, his thinning grey hair exposing a bald spot on top of his head and a bushy moustache completely covering his top lip and extending down to his jaw line on each side of his mouth. Despite the heat he wore a navy blazer over his white shirt and red tie, the bottom of which lay curled on the desk.

"Yes?" said the old man brusquely.

"I have finished for the day. Mr. Kenworthy.

"Is the job complete?"

"Another day."

41

"I thought you would be finished by now, how long does it take to redecorate?"

"The bedrooms are finished and I have done the hall ceiling and cornice. We did say four days. We also agreed half payment after two days."

"I don't remember agreeing to that, do you have it in writing?"

"No."

"Well then, let that be a lesson to you my boy, always get it in writing. I didn't build my fortune by not getting things in writing."

"It's just that I need to buy wallpaper and more paint to finish the job," said Akande nervously fidgeting with his necklace.

"Not my problem," replied Cornelius Kenworthy dismissively. "Payment on completion of job, after my inspection of course. Close the door on your way out."

Akande turned and walked dejectedly back into the hall. He knelt by his canvas holdall, closed the zip and carried it out to his van. As he drove away he wondered where he was going to get the money to finish the job. The old man had cheated him, he remembered as clear as day standing in the study when he promised to pay half the money at the midpoint. Suddenly his mind filled with resentment, he would go and see his mother, she knew exactly how to deal with the likes of Cornelius Kenworthy.

Akande climbed the stairs of the tower block. At the top he opened a discoloured door and entered a dimly lit hallway. Flickering orange light was emanating from the room at the end of the passage. He walked towards it. An old woman in a shawl sat cross-legged on the floor surrounded by candles. Light smoke rose from embers simmering on a metal bowl before her. A pole was positioned behind her on top of which was the macabre sight of a shrunken head, the eyes and mouth sewn closed. She looked up through her bedraggled hair and smiled, exposing her crooked, yellow teeth.

"You look worried, Akande. Tell me what is wrong."

"It's this new job, he will not pay the money he owes me."

"I told you not to trust him, I foresaw his character in the ashes, she said poking the embers with a thin metal needle causing a flame to rise. "He is a bad man."

"I need the money to buy more paint," he continued worriedly.

"He will be punished, Akande, maybe I put his head on a stick."

She lifted the pole and admired the shrunken head.

"I just want the money."

"Perhaps he needs some persuasion."

She reached into a wooden box and held up a small, straw doll, its arms were outstretched and it had no face.

"Bring me an item of clothing worn by this man and I will do the rest."

43

The following morning Akande pulled his van up in front of the mansion. A thin layer of snow covered the ground. He noticed a small, red car parked further along and wondered who the visitor was as he picked up his holdall and crunched his way across the gravel. Suddenly the front door flew open and a small boy rushed past him.

"Alexander! Put on your coat if you're playing outside," called a woman's voice from inside.

Akande watched as the young boy crouched down, gathering the snow and rolling it into a ball. A young, slim woman wearing an elegant navy dress appeared in the doorway carrying a small, fleecy jacket. The boy stood up gripping the snowball and pulled his arm back taking aim at his mother.

"Don't you dare throw that snowball at me," she commanded walking towards him.

He smiled mischievously, changed his aim and launched the snowball at Akande who dexterously dodged the projectile and watched it hit the ground and disintegrate.

"I'm so sorry," said the woman mortified. "He's very hyper today."

"No problem," smiled Akande.

"Apologise to the gentleman, Alexander."

But the boy was already running away. The mother set off in hot pursuit. Akande shook his head, entered the hall, put down his holdall and moved the step ladder to the rear wall.

"I expect you to be finished today," instructed Cornelius Kenworthy opening the study door.

"It will take two more days."

"Well get a move on then, I'll be working in here all day but I'll be checking on you."

The front door opened and the boy ran in and up the stairs followed by a rather distraught mother.

"Can't you keep that boy under control, Rebecca?"

"He's just playing, Dad."

"Well, get him to play quietly."

With that he closed the study door forcibly behind him.

As the sun set Akande descended the ladder. He washed his brushes and put them into the holdall before looking anxiously at the study door. The requirement for advanced payment was getting increasingly urgent. He walked slowly to the study and knocked on the door.

"Come!"

Akande entered, Cornelius Kenworthy was hunched over his desk intensely studying papers, the fire roaring.

"Thieves and swindlers, the world is full of them trying to rip me off," he raged loosening his red tie and undoing the top button of his shirt. "Have you finished?"

"I will be finished tomorrow."

"Always tomorrow, what is wrong with people these days, lazy idlers, that's what they are."

"It's just that I need to buy more paint."

"Then buy it."

"Could you advance me even £100?"

"No money until the job is complete."

"I will not be able to finish the job without more paint."

"Then no money at all, I didn't build my fortune by paying for half a job."

Suddenly, Alexander raced into the study and dived onto the rug before the fire.

"Rebecca!" yelled Cornelius Kenworthy. "Get that boy out of my study!"

Alexander completely ignored him, getting up, extending his arms and running around the room making the sound of an aeroplane. His outstretched arm clipped a vase and sent it crashing to the ground.

"Rebecca!" he yelled louder, wrenching at his tie and throwing it to the ground in annoyance.

He stood up, moved around the desk, grabbed the boy firmly by the arm and dragged him out of the study. Akande could hear him stomping up the stairs. He looked at the tie crumpled on the ground, remembering his mother's words.

"Bring me an item of clothing worn by this man and I will do the rest."

He quickly picked up the tie, stuffed it into his overalls and left.

The old woman sat cross-legged on the floor with her head bowed in the flickering candlelight. A flame danced in the metal bowl, a thin needle resting in the base, the tip buried in the burning coals. Before her, the straw man stood ominously with its arms outstretched.

"Did you get your money?" she asked looking up.

Akande shook his head solemnly.

The old woman reached into a tin beside her and handed him a wad of notes.

"Do you have it?"

Akande knelt and placed the tie on the floor. Carefully, she flattened it out with her palms then with a small, sharp, curved-bladed knife she cut a thin strip from the side. He watched silently as she deftly tied it around the neck of the doll. She closed her eyes, opened her arms and began to mutter incantations, slowly rocking back and forth. Her utterances became louder and louder, her rocking increasing speed as her arms rose steadily above her head. In the tray the fire intensified, crackling and shooting off sparks as the flames grew higher. The chanting reached fever pitch, Akande bowed his head. Suddenly she clapped her hands together high in the air and all became still and silent. The fire rescinded to a glowing ember. She removed the needle slowly from the ashes and gripped the doll firmly. The tip of the needle smouldered as she placed it against the doll's stomach. She held the needle steady, then with one strong push she pierced the doll until the

47

tip appeared through the back. The embers burst back into life and the flame burnt blood red.

"It is done, Akande, she murmured. "Tomorrow you will find the old man easier to deal with."

Akande drove anxiously to the mansion through the driving rain. Today would be the last day, he thought thankfully, he would finish the job, get his money and go. Certainly he would pay now, his mother had never failed him yet. He pulled up in front of the house and trudged through the slush into the hallway. The study door was open, Akande approached and peeked inside, the fire was lit but the old man was nowhere to be seen. Suddenly he heard footsteps on the stairs and retreated.

"I'm afraid my father is not well today, he is experiencing rather severe stomach pains," said Rebecca descending into the hall. "Do you know what you are doing?"

"Yes, I will be finished today."

"Give me a call when it is done and I will settle your bill."

Akande smiled, things were indeed going his way, the daughter would be easier to deal with than the old man. He put is holdall down and started painting around the skirting board.

About 1pm he stopped for lunch. He went into the bathroom to wash his hands. The job was almost complete, another couple of hours at most. He returned to the hall to find Alexander kneeling down and rooting around in his holdall.

"Careful, there is paint in there," he called.

The boy stood up, Akande could see the paint on his hands.

"What's going on down there," boomed a voice from the top of the stairs.

Akande looked up and saw Cornelius Kenworthy coming slowly down.

Alexander ran off into the study.

"Rebecca!" he shouted then winced and fell against the banister clutching his stomach.

"Dad? What are you doing up?"

"Get that boy out of my study," he ordered through clenched teeth.

She went into the study and emerged with Alexander.

Cornelius Kenworthy looked in horror at his hands.

"He had better not have got any paint on anything," he raged. "He took my tie yesterday."

Akande remained silent while Rebecca led the boy into the bathroom.

"Bring me some more aspirins, Rebecca," he barked before disappearing into the study and closing the door.

Two hours later Akande had cleared everything from the hall. The ladders and floor covering were back on the van and his brushes were packed in his holdall. He waited patiently for Rebecca.

"A very nice job," she complimented. "How much do we owe you?"

"£2,000."

Suddenly the study door flew open.

"One moment, Rebecca," said Cornelius Kenworthy.

Rebecca stopped writing and looked up. Cornelius Kenworthy surveyed the hall inspecting the walls.

"A bit streaky here," he appraised. "And blotchy."

"Dad, it's perfectly fine."

He looked up at the cornice.

"This seems a bit dark."

"It's the colour you requested," said Akande.

"What colour was that?"

"Ivory Silk."

"I said Ivory Lace."

"No, sir, definitely Ivory Silk."

"I'm not paying for Ivory Silk when I wanted Ivory Lace,"

"Look, I wrote it down," implored Akande taking a crumpled scrap of paper from his overalls.

"I don't care what you wrote down. Change it or I will not be settling your account," roared Cornelius Kenworthy gripping his stomach tightly and grimacing.

"Dad, you had better sit down," said Rebecca putting her arm around him and trying to lead him into the study.

"You have until tomorrow evening to fix it," he ordered as he was led away. "Fix it or no money."

The doll stood in the centre of the room, the flickering flame casting its shadow onto the wooden floor. The slither of red tie remained knotted around the neck and the long, slender needle piercing the torso. The old woman sat silently behind rotating the tip of a second needle in the glowing embers. Akande opened the door and entered with his head bowed.

"He didn't pay, did he?"

Akande shook his head.

The old woman lifted the needle and studied the light plume of smoke drifting upwards from the sharp tip.

"I knew he wouldn't."

She gripped the doll firmly and lined the needle up with the head. With one sharp thrust the tip penetrated the head and appeared through the back as the flame danced wildly and burnt red once more.

"Let's see if he is more co-operative tomorrow. This will be his last chance."

She held the pierced doll above the increasingly raging flame straining to engulf it, throwing her head back and cackling.

"Maybe I should take the doll."

"As you wish, Akande," she replied handing it to him.

Akande arrived at the mansion to find a black Mercedes parker next to the small, red car. He entered the hall just as Rebecca and a small, plump man in a dark suit and round glasses descended the stairs.

"He will be alright now, doctor, won't he?" she asked with concern.

"He will be fine, probably been working too hard, he just needs rest."

"He never usually suffers from headaches, it came on so suddenly, one moment he was fine, the nest he was clutching his head and groaning."

"You need not worry, just get him to take his medication and call me if there is no improvement by tomorrow."

"I will, thank you doctor."

As he left Rebecca rushed back up the stairs. Akande placed his holdall down and unzipped the top. Laying on top of the brushes was the doll, the two needles sticking out through the straw body. He looked at it and then gazed pensively up the stairs. Suddenly he became aware of the small boy observing him silently from the front door. Akande removed his brushes and quickly closed the bag. The boy ran past him and into the study. Akande set to work.

As darkness fell the job was complete. Akande was kneeling, placing the brushes in the holdall when he heard heavy, plodding footsteps on the stairs. He looked up as the groggy old man descended in a thick black dressing gown, his eyes bleary and his face distinctly aged.

"I have completed the job, sir," said Akande as he crossed the hall.

"Very good," murmured Cornelius Kenworthy as he craned his neck up slowly and surveyed the hall.

"There is the matter of my bill."

"Come back when this blasted headache has gone."

Cornelius Kenworthy lumbered into the study and closed the door. Akande looked pensively at the closed door then down at the doll laying in the holdall. The old man had suffered enough. He picked it up, the sharp needles piecing through the straw body. Gripping the end, he removed the lower one from the stomach, a groan emanated from the study. He took the second needle and pulled it out of the head. Behind the door he heard a heavy sigh of relief.

"It's a miracle."

The old man's voice was muffled but audible. Akande knelt down and placed the needles and doll in the bag. Perhaps he should try again to get his money. The study door opened. Akande quickly zipped up the holdall.

"Come!" ordered Cornelius Kenworthy.

His usual authoritarian demeanour had returned. Akande followed him into the study.

"Close the door," said Cornelius Kenworthy striding behind his desk.

Akande shut the door and approached. In the stone grate the fire burnt brightly, radiating heat around the room. Unseen by anyone the small boy was creeping down the stairs.

"I can't believe it, "boomed Cornelius Kenworthy. "My headache has gone as quickly as it came, my stomach cramp too."

"I'm pleased to hear it," replied Akande smiling knowingly. "Perhaps now we can settle my bill."

"Certainly."

He reached into the drawer beside him and put a bundle of notes on the desk. Akande counted it carefully.

In the hall the small boy approached the holdall and opened the zip. On top lay the doll. He looked at it quizzically. It was a strange looking toy. He ran his finger along the torn red strip around the neck. Quickly he grabbed it and raced up the stairs.

"There is only £1000 here," said Akande. "We agreed £2000."

"That was before the mistakes."

"What mistakes?"

"The wrong paint colour, Ivory Silk for Ivory Lace."

"I changed that at my own expense."

"Then there is the issue of the job over-running, it was supposed to be four days and took five."

"That was due to having to change the paint."

"I'm not interested in excuses, there are always penalties for late work."

Akande looked at the bundle of notes.

"Take it or leave it," said Cornelius Kenworthy smiling arrogantly. "We can always settle it in court. Can you afford to go to court?"

Akande looked at the old man with contempt. He snatched up the bundle of notes and walked hurriedly across the room, throwing the door open, grabbing his holdall and heading for his van. He revved the engine, spaying gravel from the spinning rear wheels as he sped away. Cornelius Kenworthy watched from the study window and chortled heartily, he hadn't acquired his wealth by not playing hard ball. Suddenly the small boy raced into the study.

"Stop that running," bellowed Cornelius Kenworthy.

Alexander stopped dead in his tracks and looked up at his scowling face.

"I told you I don't want you in here."

Cornelius Kenworthy strode towards him. Alexandre bolted around the desk and scrambled underneath.

"Rebecca! Get this boy out of here!" he bawled approaching the desk.

Alexander popped his head out, the old man grabbed him by the back of his collar and dragged him out, the doll falling from the small boy's hand.

"He's just playing, Dad," said Rebecca appearing in the doorway. "Don't be so rough with him."

"Take him home."

"Fine. Come on Alexander."

She took him by the hand and led him out. Cornelius Kenworthy lifted the decanter from the desk and poured himself a large brandy. He went to the window and watched the car drive away into the darkness. Peace at last, he thought, not a bad day at all. He took a sip and smiled smugly in satisfaction, he had got rid of that little brat and saved himself £1000 on painting and decoration. That had been a stroke of genius with the hall paint, he knew he had asked for Ivory Silk paint on the cornice but once it was done he could see it was too dark and Ivory Lace would be better. It was simplicity itself to tell Akande the mistake was his, furthermore the lad had to change the paint at his own cost, genius. He took another sip and warmed himself on the fire before returning to the desk. Sat down he felt something under his foot. He bent down and picked up the object studying it carefully. What an ugly doll, he thought. He rotated it looking disparagingly at the woven straw and strip of red material around the neck. It must belong to that urchin, typical of him to have such a cheap, nasty looking doll, it didn't even have a face. A smirk spread across his face as he looked at the doll and then the fire. The boy needed a lesson and he would give him one. He finished the brandy and walked slowly to the grate. The flames roared up the chimney. He took a last glance at the doll and tossed it into the fire.

Akande turned the key in the lock and entered his small flat. He dropped the holdall in the hall and for the first time noticed it was open, he was certain he had closed it before he left the mansion.

"Akande!"

He left the bag and walked to the dimly lit room at the end of the passage. The old woman was in her usual position on the floor.

"Did you get your money, Akande?"

"I got half of it."

"He is a bad man, don't do any more jobs for him. I will take back the doll."

Akande returned to the hall and knelt by the holdall. He opened it wide and scanned for the doll. Where was it, he had put it on top. Frantically he began pulling out brushes and rags until the bag was empty.

"It's gone," he said desperately returning to his mother.

"Did you remove the red tie?"

"No."

"You must get it back, Akande. The doll is still enchanted as long as it remains around the neck."

Akande raced out of the flat, he knew all too well the power of Voodoo. He got in his van and sped up the road.

As he neared the mansion, he could see the smoke drifting up over the treetops. In front of the smouldering building sat fire engines, a police car and an ambulance with their light. Akande stopped the van and dismounted. He moved closer looking in horror at the scene. Beside him the chief fireman took out his phone.

"It's unclear what caused the fire, but it seems to have started in the study, the charred remains were found of one person, we believe it's the owner, Cornelius Kenworthy."

WHATEVER IT TAKES

Tim looked down at the familiar red surface before his eyes followed the two white lines that narrowed in the distance. He was barely aware of the sun beating down on his exposed skin or the constant cheering from the surrounding stadium. A fast start was imperative, it was his only chance.

"Tim Hudson."

He became aware of his name being announced, glancing up momentarily, raising his hand and waving to the crowd then quickly lowering it and staring back down the track.

"Steven Johnson."

The stadium erupted, this was the person they had all come to see. He stood God-like in the middle lane, his muscular arms glistening, his yellow vest hugging his defined torso, with the word "Jamaica" proudly emblazoned on the front. His trademark golden chains resplendent around his neck. Even Tim could not ignore the enveloping cacophony. Steven Johnson, the single reason why he had a box in his garage full of silver medals. He had to start fast, he just had to.

"Gary Springer."

The new American hope, younger, bigger and still not at his peak, but developing at an alarming rate. He waved to the cheering crowd, displaying his pearly white teeth as he smiled magnanimously, running his hand through his wavy, blonde hair. Tim briefly looked at him, he was no threat, at least, not yet.

"Take your marks."

Tim crouched down and moved his foot back, placing it carefully on the block before locating the other. He placed his hands behind the white line, the only thing he could see was the finish line.

"Set."

The stadium hushed into an expectant silence. He raised from his knee and tensed his body, waiting for one single sound. He exploded out of the blocks as the gun shot resounded around the stadium. His arms and legs pumped as his feet hammered along the ground, his body rising, no-one in his peripheral vision. The finish becoming closer and closer with each stride. This was his time. His body began to decelerate as he approached the finish, to his right he suddenly glimpsed a hint of yellow. He crossed the line and doubled over with his hands on his knees, breathing heavily. He looked up at the giant scoreboard, a personal best, he slumped to the ground and watched as Steven Johnson draped a Jamaican flag over his shoulders and took the enthusiastic accolades from the crowd. What more could he do? He trudged wearily into the changing room.

Opening the locker he removed his bag and took out the clear plastic water bottle. He looked at the familiar label, a red lightning bolt shooting into a snow covered mountain peak with the name above, "Pure Ice Water." They seemed to sponsor every race he was at now. On the television above he could see the winner being interviewed. His eyes narrowed as his grip tightened on the bottle, unscrewing the lid and tossing it to the ground before raising it to his lips and taking a sharp gulp.

"Congratulations, Tim, a personal best."

He looked at his compatriot and smiled weakly. Gary stopped beside him and looked at the screen,

"He's a great champion, the fastest man who ever lived."

Tim took another swig from the bottle.

"He won't be around much longer, not at his age, the rumours are this summer's Olympics will be his last."

"Mine too, the future is yours Gary, third today, a good chance of repeating the feat in the Olympics."

"I'm expecting to do better than that."

Tim looked at the steely determination in the young man's eyes.

An official entered the room.

"Follow me please, gentlemen."

They followed the official along the corridor into the drug testing room.

The Olympics came around fast, the athletes' village was full of nationalities from all over the world, from the well represented countries, like the USA and China, to the lesser so, like Dominica and Tuvalu.

Tim lay on the small, single bed with his eyes closed, his mind concentrated on the earlier race. Yes, he had won his semi-final, yes, this would assure him a good lane for tomorrow night's final, yes, it was sub-ten seconds. Yet it was still a slower time than Steven Johnson. Why did he have to be in the same era as Steven Johnson? If he had been born ten years earlier or ten years later he would have Olympic gold by now, maybe even two, or three. His thoughts were disturbed by a gentle knock on the door. He opened his eyes and glanced at the bedside clock then through the window at the darkness, his brow furrowed as he looked back at the door. Again came the soft tapping on the wood. He pushed himself up and moved cautiously to the door and opened it.

"Gary? Do you know what time it is?"

"I have to speak with you," he said quietly glancing furtively along the corridor.

"Make it quick," replied Tim returning to the bed.

Gary entered swiftly, closing and locking the door. Tim scrutinised him as he sat in the chair opposite.

"It's about the final tomorrow, do you think you can win?"

Tim remained silent and looked up at the ceiling, a small spider was making its way slowly across the tiles.

"I can guarantee you will," whispered Gary.

Tim turned his head towards him and watched aa he produced a small vial from his jacket pocket. Inside was a clear liquid.

"What's that?"

"This is the ticket to gold, engineered androstenedione."

"Drugs, are you crazy? That will be picked up immediately by the drugs test, I'm not taking it and neither should you."

"I know that, it's not for us."

Tim sat up and stared at him.

"Who's it for then?"

"Steven Johnson."

"Steven Johnson?"

"That's right. It's unlikely we can beat Johnson, especially after his time in today, The only alternative is to ensure he is disqualified."

"You're insane."

"This is your last chance for an Olympic gold medal, in four years you will be declining, if you are still competing at all."

Tim gazed up at the spider, it had stopped moving and remained motionless.

"How do you intend to get Johnson to take it?"

"Come to my room and I'll show you."

Gary opened the door quietly and looked in both directions, all was still. The two men made their way stealthily along the corridor to Gary's room. Once inside he picked up the small desk and placed it in the middle of the room. He then went to the wardrobe, knelt down and removed a small, square case from under a pile of clothes. Tim observed him through narrow, questioning eyes as he placed it carefully on the table and turned the dials on the combination lock. The clasps sprung up and he opened the lid to reveal a bottle of Pure Ice water lying on its side, a small tube of glue, a syringe and a strange tool with a round wooden handle from which protruded a long thin spike that narrowed at the end into a sharp tip. Gary removed the contents and placed them on the desk. Carefully he picked up the tool.

"What's that?" asked Tim.

"An awl, it's for making a hole in the water bottle."

He reached into his pocket and placed the vial down beside the syringe.

"You will need to hold the bottle upside down so I can puncture a hole in the bottom."

"What about fingerprints?"

"No-one will check the bottle."

"I'm not taking any chances."

He walked across to the sink and took a small towel from the rail. Returning to the table he wrapped the towel around the bottle and turned it upside down. Gary picked up the awl and gently placed the tip in the centre groove on the bottom. He pushed gently down on the awl. The plastic held firm. He increased the pressure until he felt the tip pierce the base. Carefully he removed it and placed it back down on the table. Tim watched as a bead of water dripped from the tip. Gary unscrewed the lid of the vial and put the syringe into the liquid. The syringe filled with the drug. He moved the syringe to the bottle, carefully inserting the tip into the hole. He squeezed the handle and the syringe emptied its contents inside. Finally, he squeezed a tiny blob of glue onto the tip of the awl and smeared it onto the hole.

"Just hold the bottle until the glue hardens."

Gary took the syringe and awl to the sink and rinsed them under the tap.

"How are you going to get this bottle to Johnson?"

"The sponsors water is set up on the table just inside the dressing room and Johnson always takes the bottle closest to the first locker, so that's where I will place it."

"What if he doesn't take the bottle nearest the locker this time?"

"He will."

"What if he doesn't?"

"There's always an element of risk."

"What if the bottle is examined for drugs?"

"No-one is going to check the sponsors' water."

"What if they do?"

"No-one can trace it back to us."

"Your fingerprints are all over it."

"That's how confident I am no one will examine the bottle, besides, I have to position it, it would draw unnecessary attention if I am seen wearing gloves at the height of summer."

Tim looked uncertainly at the bottle while Gary replaced the equipment back into the case, locked it and replaced it back at the bottom of the wardrobe piling the clothes back on top.

"It should be hard by now."

He lifted up the bottle, gave it a vigorous shake and inspected it."

"Perfect, you can't even see it."

"You can see the glue on the base."

"Only if you look closely and who is going to do that?"

Tim stared at the hard blob of glue and bit his lower lip, he could see it.

"When will you do it.?"

"Tomorrow, just before the final."

He moved the desk back to the wall and stood the bottle upright in the centre.

"Don't worry, nothing will go wrong, by this time tomorrow you will have the gold medal."

Tim tossed and turned in his bed in a semi-slumbering state as the sun's rays began to filter into the room. Visions of Johnson drinking from the spiked bottle and thoughts of its repercussions filled his mind. The press hounding Johnson in the aftermath, the lurid stories casting doubt on all his previous achievements, turning a great athlete into a pariah. His thoughts changed to an image of himself stood on the podium, a gleaming gold medal around his neck, standing proudly below the stars and stripes flag as the Star-Spangled Banner played. A smile of contentment emerged on his face as he drifted into sleep.

In Gary's room the curtains were drawn, in the centre of the desk the bottle stood ominously in the dim light. He picked it up and placed it into his holdall, walking out through the door oblivious to the small droplet of water that lay motionless in the middle of the desk. The corridor to the finalists' changing room was deserted, outside, in the arena, he could her the crowd cheering. He moved stealthily along the passage, suddenly a door opened, making him stop dead. An official stepped out and walked briskly towards him. Gary smiled weakly as he approached, but the official barely looked at him as he sped past and disappeared around the corner. Gary listened as his footsteps became fainter and fainter. He let out a deep breath and moved further down the corridor until he stood facing the finalists room door. Lowering his hand to the knob he turned it slowly and eased it open. The room was tranquil, he looked at the rows of bottles arranged neatly on the table. Swiftly he placed his bag on the ground, removed the bottle and switched it with the one nearest the locker. He put the switched bottle in the bag, zipped it up and departed as quickly as he had come.

Tim sat on the edge of his bed, holding his phone in both hands on his lap. He stared tensely at the screen. Maybe he should contact Gary, call the whole thing off. He slung the mobile onto the bed and crossed the room to the sink, turning the tap The water gushed down, he lowered his head and splashed it over his face before looking at his reflection in the mirror. He clenched his jaw and steeled his eyes, it was the only way. A sudden bleep emanated behind him. He moved quickly and picked up the phone, one short text, "It's done."

The noise in the stadium was increasing as the time for the final everyone had come to see drew near. Tim walked slowly along the passage, he could hear the bustle emanating from the finalists dressing room. He entered silently, and approached the table apprehensively, the bottle nearest the locker was still there. Gary sat on a bench watching him. Tim snatched up a bottle moved across the room and sat beside him, neither man speaking. He placed the bottle down between them and began to remove his kit from his bag, looking up as Steven Johnson entered with compatriot Henry Thorn. Johnson moved to the table and extended his hand towards the bottle. Tim was transfixed as his hand neared the bottle. Suddenly, Thorn reached across him and snatched it.

"I think I'll take this bottle, it seems to bring you good luck," he said.

"Give me that," demanded Johnson.

"No, I think it must have some magic power."

Tim looked anxiously at the scene

"Give me that bottle, repeated Johnson more forcefully.

Thorn dropped his bag and held the bottle up, waving it provocatively. Johnson lunged forward but he moved deftly to the side.

"I'm not joking, give me that bottle."

His face was becoming more irate by the second.

"What's it worth?" teased Thorn moving further back.

Johnson sped towards him stepping on Thorn's dropped bag and collapsing suddenly on the ground clenching his left ankle.

"You idiot," he hissed through his pained expression. "Get the physio."

Thorn dropped the bottle and ran from the changing room. The bottle rolled under the bench as Johnson clutched his ankle which was already visibly swelling. Tim got up and knelt down beside him.

70

"It looks like you've twisted it," he observed.

The physio rushed into the changing room. All eyes were on the scene as he removed Johnson's trainer and sock. While he inspected the ankle and everyone looked on anxiously Gary bent quietly down and picked up the water bottle.

"You've torn the ligaments." diagnosed the physio.

"It's the final," cried Johnson in despair. "Can't you do something for me?"

"I'm afraid not."

Johnson looked down at his swollen ankle dejectedly. The physio helped him to his feet and escorted him hobbling from the room.

Tim sat slowly down on the bench, closed his eyes and tilted his head back. He let out a sigh and felt the tension lift from his body. He could now win gold authentically, without cheating, without ruining a champion's reputation. Suddenly, he felt unexpected for sympathy for Johnson, prevented from retaining his title. It was not his fault he had to withdraw and now he was the favourite. He took a swig from his water bottle and looked around the room. Gary was fast but not as fast as him, there was no-one else who could realistically challenge him. He moved his head close to Gary and whispered.

"Did you get the bottle?"

"It's all taken care of," he replied patting his holdall.

"They are ready for you now," announced an official from the doorway.

Tim stood up, this was it.

The arena was packed with fans, the noise deafening as the athletes walked out under the floodlights onto the track and took their places. Tim looked at the empty lane beside him then down to the finishing line. Suddenly, the floodlights were switched off casting the stadium into darkness. The track lit up as rays of light shot along its length. Tim felt a sense of exhilaration as the music boomed all around him. He was about to embark on the most important ten seconds of his life. Ten seconds that would shape his future, ten seconds that would put him in the record books, ten seconds that would give him the one thing he had dreamt about all his life.

The floodlights burst back into life, as the crowd went into a deafening rapture all around.

"Take your marks."

The arena went dramatically silent. This was it, his heart began to beat faster as he felt his mouth dry.

"Set."

Everything disappeared from his mind, the crowd, the other runners, all he could see was a red strip to the finish line surrounded by an otherwise black universe.

The shot exploded like a cannon in his mind and he felt his body driving forward. The roar of the crowd was like thunder as he accelerated down the track. He was alone, the line getting closer and closer. In the corner of his eye he glimpsed a red vest, Gary Springer. He only had to hold on for another few metres. The noise in the stadium reached fever pitch, he dipped his chest as he surged over the finishing line, collapsing exhausted. He looked up at the scoreboard, had he done it? The scoreboard was blank. Time seemed to stand still, after all this was he beaten on the line? Was he destined to never win Olympic gold. The scoreboard came to life, first, winning time, 9.79 seconds, Tim Hudson. He staggered to his feet and just stared at his name at the top of the board, his eyes sparkling and his mouth open. After all these years, Tim Hudson, Olympic champion. He felt a strong hand grip his and shake it vigorously.

"Well done, Tim."

"Thanks, Henry, " he mumbled, dazed as he tried to comprehend the momentousness of the occasion.

He looked all around at the cheering crowd. This was real, Olympic gold. He walked across the track and picked up an American flag that had been thrown down to him. Draped in the stars and stripes he jogged along in front of the stand, savouring the adulation of the crowd, he wanted to remember this moment forever. One last wave and he entered the tunnel.

"This way for the drugs test Mr; Hudson," said an official leading him down a narrow corridor.

Back in his room he lay on the bed, a seemingly eternal smile painted on his face. In the hall he could hear excited voices, the only word he could make out was "disqualified." He got up slowly, crossed the room and opened the door. A small group of athletes was gathered further down the hall.

"What's going on?" he called.

"There's a rumour someone has been disqualified for failing a drugs test."

"Who?"

"We don't know, but it's someone big."

Tim went back into his room, he looked through the window, below he could see television crews, photographers and members of the press assembling. It could not be anything to do with him, he had always been clean. Had someone drunk from the bottle they had spiked. No, it couldn't be, Gary had taken it when Johnson fell. In the corridor he could hear heavy footsteps approaching. They were getting louder and louder. Abruptly, they stopped. Tim held his breath and listened. Suddenly, he was shocked by a sharp rap at his door. With his heart accelerating he crossed the room and opened it. He came face to face with three stern looking officials.

"Tim Hudson you have failed the drugs test and have been disqualified from the 100m final."

"I've failed the drugs test?" spluttered Tim dazed. "I've never taken drugs in my life."

"Traces of the banned substance androstenedione were found in your sample. The gold medal will now be awarded to Gary Springer."

They turned briskly and retreated down the hall. Tim let the door close as he staggered back and slumped down on the bed. This was not possible. He removed the water bottle from his bag and took a long drink. There must be a mistake. Suddenly he felt a drop of water land on his bare thigh. He lowered the bottle from his lips and looked at it quizzically. A second droplet fell from the bottom of the bottle, landing beside the first. He screwed the lid back on and turned the bottle upside down. He stared in horror at the small blob of glue.

THE CAMP

"Come on, Harold, just three more."

Harold could feel the sick rising in his stomach, would he be able to get through this torment or find himself lying in his own vomit. He dropped down, placing his hands on the grass and shuffled his feet back slowly. Breathing heavily he dragged them forward and stood up.

"Jump up, Harold, jump up. You're doing burpees not getting out of bed."

Harold gave a limp jump causing his distended stomach to wobble beneath the sweat soaked vest. Vomitees would be a more accurate description he thought as he dropped back down and just remained static on his hands and knees staring at the ground.

"Do you want to lose weight or not?"

Yes, of course he did, why else would he put himself through this torture. No-one would put themselves through this agony voluntarily, those that do should be locked up. He would definitely campaign to have exercise banned when he returned to Omaha, especially bloody burpees. He staggered to his feet and tried to jump but his feet remained firmly affixed to the grass.

"Last one, Harold."

He lowered his weary body for the final time. Surely there was some human rights law against this level of punishment. Feeling increasingly nauseas he struggled to his feet and placed his hands on his knees with his head down, panting heavily.

"That's all for now, you'll need to work harder next time, Harold."

Harold looked up at his tormentor, his face seemed to have been carved out of granite with his chiselled jaw and dark, sunken eyes. The first day he arrived at the camp in the Nebraska wilderness and saw him he just knew he was one of these guys who lived for exercise. Always dressed in camouflage trousers and a dark green vest to expose his gorilla like arms. No doubt he would have loved to have been an army drill sergeant if it was not for his criminal past. Most people would be ashamed of a penal record but not Jim Stretton, no, he took pride in serving time, made a man of him as he took satisfaction in stating. Harold wondered how exactly he had got to own, when all is said, a fat camp. He certainly had no intention of telling anybody he had been to a fat camp when this was all over. This was his last throw of the dice in an effort to lose weight and hopefully turn his life around. He trudged towards the others sat around the wooden table outside the converted barn which was his home for the foreseeable future.

He slumped down still breathing heavily.

"The first day is always the toughest," said the older man opposite him. "Isn't that right, Bethany."

The plump woman beside him nodded.

"Too true, Derek. Sadly it doesn't get much easier."

"Does he need to be so extreme?" panted Harold.

"That's Jim Stretton for you, ex-marine," replied Derek.

Harold just knew it, he was only surprised they did not have to yell "SIR, YES, SIR."

"What's for lunch?" asked Harold slowly recovering his breath. "Pizza with all the toppings would go down well right now."

The woman opposite laughed and nodded in agreement.

"Lentil soup, it's always lentil soup on Tuesday," said Derek..

Harold looked at them both, surprised that the bench could support their combined weight. They made him feel better about his own size, but he knew that was the reason they were all here.

"Split-pea soup tomorrow," continued Derek. "You'll find there's a lot of soup served here."

"And salad," added Bethany.

A slim woman approached them from the farmhouse carrying a tray. She placed it on the table and put a bowl of soup before each of them.

"Any rolls? asked Harold.

She looked at him scornfully.

"No bread for you," she said sternly. "Remember why you are here."

She moved away briskly.

"That's, Jim's wife, Mary, she exudes all the warmth of an ice lolly at the Arctic Circle," observed Derek..

Harold looked at the meagre bowl of soup, dipping his spoon in and swirling it about. He put it in his mouth, and screwed up his face, lukewarm and disgusting. He had only arrived last night and was already beginning to regret it. The sleeping quarters were in the barn behind. Small rooms with a single metal framed bed and a lumpy mattress on top. An old wooden wardrobe and that was it. If you stood in the middle of the room with your arms outstretched you could almost touch the side walls with your fingertips.. Harold was surprised they had not made him wear an orange boiler suit.

Bethany and Derek had been at the camp for a few weeks and knew the routine well.

"I thought there would be more of us," said Harold spooning in the soup before it got any colder.

"There was a woman, Sheila, when I arrived, really big woman, but she managed to escape," said Derek.

Escape seemed to be an appropriate word. The camp was really just a converted farm in the wilderness.. It had been difficult for Harold to find when he had driven here yesterday. He lost all satellite connection miles out to navigate his car. That was one of the features of the camp, no access to the outside world. When he arrived Jim Streeton had met him. He had shown him to his room and taken his car keys, another rule of the camp. It was a full commitment to the programme. Nobody left until they had achieved their agreed weight loss.

"Did she achieve her target weight loss?" asked Harold tilting the bowl and scraping the last remnants of soup from the bottom.

"Who?"

"This woman, Sheila."

"No, if anything she gained weight."

"How did she manage to put on weight?"

"Don't know, I don't seem to be losing any myself."

"So, how come she was allowed to leave?"

"They must have given up on her, I suppose. I woke up one morning and Jim said she had left in the night. Must have done, I noticed her car was gone. It was the same night they had a party in the farmhouse, some friends of Jim and Mary arrived in the afternoon. An odd mix of people, I thought I recognised one of them, but I can't remember where from."

He stopped speaking abruptly as Mary Stretton suddenly appeared at the table.

She placed small cups in front of Harold and Derek. Harold looked inside at the small white pills.

"What are these? he asked.

"They will help you lose weight," she replied dryly.

He watched as Derek emptied the contents into his mouth.

"Are you not taking any, Bethany?" asked Harold.

"No, I'm allergic to them."

Harold looked doubtfully at the pills. He was not a big believer in taking medication, still if it got results. He shrugged his shoulders and swallowed them all.

"Better get some rest before this afternoons activity," she said picking up the empty bowls and walking away.

"This afternoon's activity?" queried Harold in disbelief. "I thought that was it for the day."

"Not by a long way," replied Derek getting up and moving towards the barn followed by Bethany.

Harold ambled wearily to his feet and called after them as he traipsed slowly to the barn.

"What's this afternoon?"

"A hike."

Harold stopped and his shoulders slumped as he watched them disappear inside. A hike? He trudged to the barn and went inside. There was a narrow corridor with four numbered doors in a row. He could hear Bethany moving about in the first room, room 2 was the communal bathroom, room 3 was vacant and he watched Derek going into room 4. At the end of the corridor was a spiral staircase leading to the upper level.

Harold climbed the stairs wearily wishing he was on the ground floor. He did not know why he could not be on the ground floor, room 3 was vacant. At the top of the stairs he looked down the windowless corridor, a strip light in the ceiling midway along providing dim illumination. Oddly the rooms were numbered in the opposite direction going from number five nearest the stairs. Typical, his room would have to be the end one. He dragged his exhausted and stiff body along to his door and opened it. There was a lock but no key. Not very big on security, he thought, not that he had brought anything worth stealing, and they were in the middle of nowhere. He opened the door and entered the tiny room. It was so narrow he bet if he stood in the middle he could almost touch the side walls. The sun streamed through the window. He closed the thin curtains which barely reduced the light and turned towards the small thin metal bed. The rusted legs went into discoloured rubber stoppers. He trudged wearily to it and dropped down heavily. The metal frame creaked and he felt the lumpy mattress below his back but was too tired to care. The only other furniture was an old wooden wardrobe at the edge of the bed in which he had put his clothes and belongings before cramming his suitcase under the bed. He picked up his phone, no signal, same as last night when he arrived. This place was remote, cut off both geographically and technologically. He placed it down on the floor and looked up at the bare light bulb hanging by an exposed wire from the ceiling. Would it even be safe to turn on he pondered chewing on his lower lip disconcertedly. It would all be worth it if he could lose weight he reassured himself. He closed his eyes and fell into a deep sleep.

He was woken abruptly by a loud banging on his door. The bed creaked as he sat up in a state of disorientation.

"Get up, Harold," barked Jim opening the door. "Time for afternoon hike. Be downstairs in five minutes."

With that he slammed the door shut making the room shake. Harold sat on the edge of the bed and rubbed his eyes, feeling like he had only just got into bed. Maybe the fresh air would liven him up he thought optimistically, if doubtfully.

Outside Derek and Bethany were waiting in caps, shorts and t-shirts and carrying small rucksacks on their backs

"I am unable to get a signal on my phone."

"No, there is none anywhere around here," replied Derek.

"Nothing?"

"No, no Wi Fi, no calls or messages."

"So, we are completely cut off."

"That's how they want it, so we can concentrate totally on losing weight."

"Take this," instructed Jim appearing and handing him a backpack. "You're cap is inside."

Harold opened the top and looked inside at the cap. a bottle of water and a jar of pills.

"What are the pills for?"

"Hydration, it gets pretty hot out there."

Harold picked up the jar, no label, they looked very similar to the ones he had taken after lunch.

"Stop staring at them and put the bag on your back, Harold. We want to get off."

He put the cap on his head and they set off along the dusty road with the sun beating down on them. His t-shirt was already beginning to stick to his body with the sweat, if it was so hot why were they going in the middle of the afternoon at peak heat, he pondered. They left the road and took a trail towards the hills. At least the trees provided some shade from the sun. As they started the gradual ascent Harold had dropped to the rear.

"Keep up, Harold," shouted Jim from the front.

Harold panted as he caught up with Bethany.

"How far are we going?" he murmured between gasps.

"It's usually a couple of hours."

Harold wiped the perspiration from his forehead wondering how he was going to survive the first day.

The trail was getting steeper as they wound their way upwards and the trees denser. Harold had become detached at the back once more. Bethany had caught up with Jim further ahead and he could see them chatting in the distance as they walked. Derek was waiting for him sitting on a shaded rock sipping from his water bottle.

"I don't think I can do it," gasped Harold clambering up to him and dropping to his knees.

"The first one is always the worst. Take a rehydration pill."

Harold removed his backpack and tipped a pill into his hand.

"These look the same as the weight loss pills," he remarked scrutinising it.

"I thought that too but Jim said all pills look the same, I suppose he's right."

Harold put the pill in his mouth and washed it down with a gulp of water before drinking thirstily.

"Save some for later, Harold."

He put the water back inside and picked up the rucksack. Suddenly, he stopped, something caught his eye in the coarse grass below the rock. He reached down and removed it, it was a bracelet of coloured gemstones of red, green, blue and yellow.

"What have you got there?" asked Derek.

"It's a bracelet."

"Let me see."

Harold handed him the bracelet. Derek looked at it closely.

"It's a Chakra bracelet."

"Chakra?"

"Yes, supposedly the different gemstones show your personality and have spiritual properties. For example, the red gemstone is the root Chakra, it preserves and replenishes life."

"Are you into this type of thing?"

"No, Sheila used to go on and on about it, she believed in all this spirituality nonsense."

"She sounds like quite a character."

"Oh, she was, she would sit with her legs crossed in the rising sun early in the morning surrounded by a circle of coloured gemstones supposedly in a meditative trance. She used to wear a necklace with a dragonfly pendent that had Chakra gemstones in the wings and tail. Funnily enough she used to stay in the room you are in."

He paused and studied the bracelet.

"This bracelet looks very much like one she used to wear."

"We're waiting for you," said Jim suddenly appearing. "What have you got there?"

"I think this belongs to Sheila," said Derek showing it to him. "Strange though, we never hiked this route before."

"We must have done it before you arrived,"

"I can send it back to her. What's her address?"

"There's no need, "said Jim taking the bracelet.

"I'm sure she will want it back."

"I doubt it, it's not very valuable."

"More for its spiritual value rather than its price."

"Fine. I'll see she gets it," he said shoving it into bis pocket. "Now let's get off."

He strode purposefully up towards Bethany.

Harold put his rucksack back on and stared up the hill. Looking back over his shoulder Derek was studying the ground intensely.

"Get a move on, Derek," yelled Jim.

Derek looked at him, his eyes narrowed as he concentrated on what had just happened.

****

Harold collapsed onto the bench, his arms crossed on the table and resting his body against them. His legs ached, his back ached and his feet hurt. This was only the first day.

"I'll be glad to get to bed," he said listlessly. "And I still have to climb those stairs. I'm going to ask for a room on the ground floor, number three is obviously free."

"It's being used as a storeroom," said Bethany.

"There must be other places they can store stuff, this is a farm after all."

"Sheila had asked to move too but to no avail," added Derek.

"You'd think they would want the room for other people," grumbled Harold. "They can't make much money with only three of us."

He glanced across to the farmhouse. Jim was sat in the porch sipping from a glass while a bottle of bourbon stood on the table beside him..

"He does that every night," said Derek following his gaze. "He'll be drunk later."

"He wasn't drunk last night when I arrived late."

"Almost every night then."

"But he did take my car keys."

"That's to ensure you don't up and leave in the middle of the night."

Harold watched as Mary descended the porch steps carrying a tray and crossed the grass towards them.

"What's tonight?" asked Harold as she placed it on the table.

"Pasta, Cannellini Beans with Bell Peppers and Zucchini," she replied dryly turning and walking briskly away.

Harold looked at the dry unappetising food, not caring as he shovelled it hungrily into his mouth.

"It was funny finding Sheila's bracelet today," said Derek.

"It might not have been hers," replied Bethany.

"Come on, who else around here would wear a Chakra bracelet like that."

"Ok. Maybe it was hers," conceded Bethany.

"Then when did she lose it? I remember she was wearing it the day before she left."

"Maybe she had more than one."

"Maybe," said Derek deep in thought. "I've never been that way. Have you hiked it before?"

"No,"

"I mean before I arrived?"

"No."

"Then how did it get there?"

Bethany paused, looking up at Jim, his piercing eyes meeting hers.

"I don't know. Maybe she went up there alone."

"Jim would never allow that. You know we can't leave the camp. That's why they take our car keys when we arrive. We're imprisoned here."

Bethany fell silent, lowering her face and stirring her fork in the pasta.

Jim gulped down the contents of his glass, wiped his arm across his mouth and staggered down from the porch. He crossed the grass unsteadily and approached the group.

"That was a slow hike today, you'll need to be quicker next time," he slurred.

"You mean tomorrow," mumbled Derek.

"No, there'll be no hike tomorrow, we have some friends coming to stay. You have the afternoon off."

The group gave a collective sigh of relief.

"Is it the same ones as last time?" asked Derek.

"Yea that's right. Harold, did you find a key in your room?"

"No, but I was wondering where the key was, I'd like to be able to lock the room."

"Ah, don't worry about that, there are no thieves out here. Besides, it's not the key to your room."

"What's it the key for then?"

"Jim, go back to the house."

Mary suddenly appeared steering him away from the group.

"They are an odd couple," observed Harold as he watched them go back to the farmhouse."

"Wait until you meet their friends tomorrow," said Derek dryly.

****

"Come on, Harold, put some effort into it."

Harold placed the block of wood upright on the block. Breathing heavily he raised the axe wearily above his head. Struggling to focus he wielded the axe down, splitting the wood in two. The blade embedded in the block. He put his foot on the block and wrenched it out. The sun beat down on him as he placed the next piece on the block. Bethany and Derek were sat on the bench recovering. Why was he always last? He sliced the wood in half.

"Last one, Harold."

Harold positioned the last piece. With one last effort he brought the axe down watching the two halves fall to the ground. He left the blade implanted in the block and traipsed to the bench, relieved it was all over.

"That wood will keep us going for a while," said Jim. "Might as well benefit from your efforts today. I'll get the scales."

He put the wood into a wheelbarrow and took it to the farmhouse.

"I'm not looking forward to this weigh in," said Derek looking at his large stomach. "I think I've gained weight, not lost it."

"You'll be fine," said Bethany encouragingly.

Derek seemed doubtful as Jim returned carrying an old set of scales.

"Right Derek, you can go first," said Jim placing it on the ground.

Derek got up and stepped onto the scales.

"200 pounds," announced Jim. "3 less than last week."

"Well done," gushed Bethany.

"I don't feel lighter," said Derek doubtfully.

"Oh, you definitely look better," she added.

"Ok. Bethany."

Bethany stepped on the scales.

"Well done," said Jim. "150 pounds, 10 lost."

Bethany smiled radiantly.

That is incredible, thought Harold, he would not have thought it was possible to lose 10 pounds in a week. She did not even take the pills. Maybe the diet and exercise here really was miraculous. Despite only being here for two days perhaps he would see some huge losses too he thought optimistically. He stepped onto the scales.

"First weigh in, Harold, 220 lbs," advised Jim.

"That's incredible, I weighed in the day before I came here at 230 lbs. Are you sure those scales are right?"

"You're being too hard on yourself, Harold. Look how hard you've been working," said Bethany.

"I suppose so, but still, 10 pounds."

He was interrupted by the roar of an engine. They looked towards the farm entrance, coming down the lane trailing a dust cloud behind was a huge motorbike. It stopped alongside Harold's car and the rider dismounted removing his helmet to reveal his long, dark, oily hair. As he sauntered towards the group Harold observed the scar along his left cheek from his ear to the corner of his mouth. His leather jacket was etched in dust and grime. He shook hands firmly with Jim Stretton.

"Good to see you, Larry," said Jim. "I'll get you a beer."

"You're new here, ain't you," he said looking at Harold.

"Yes," replied Harold disconcertedly looking at his yellow-stained teeth.

"Larry Dwyer," he said shaking his hand.

He removed his jacket to expose the black tattoo of a scorpion on his forearm. Harold stared at it.

"Nice, ain't it," said Larry. "It's my birth sign. You got any tattoos?"

"No,"

"What's wrong, you too afraid to get one done?"

"No, it never really appealed to me."

"Everyone has them where I come from."

"Where's that?"

"Just outside Beaumont, Texas."

"That's a long bike ride."

"Near enough 1000 miles."

"Why didn't you fly, there are flights from Houston to Omaha?"

"I'll never fly again."

"Larry, I got your beer," shouted Jim from the porch. "Come on over."

"Later folks."

Larry headed up to the farmhouse.

Harold was glad there was no hike today. His body was getting sorer and sorer. He sat at the table and played cards with Derek in the evening when a gleaming silver Mercedes came along the track and parked next to the motorbike. Out stepped a distinguished looking grey haired man in a navy suit. They watched as he went up the stairs to the porch and shook hands with Larry. Harold looked on in astonishment, the contrast between the two men could not have been more striking.

"This is an odd collection of people," observed Harold.

"I told you. They were here last month," replied Derek. "The new guy is Thomas Buchanan."

"Thomas Buchanan?" I thought I recognised him. "He was on television."

"For what?"

"He had been one of the survivors of a plane crash in the Andes last year. It was two months before they were rescued. There were over 200 people on the flight, it was a miracle anyone survived, I believe there were only five."

Jim came over to the group.

"There is going to be a bit of a party tonight," he said.

"What's the party for?" asked Harold.

"Oh, it's Larry's birthday."

He walked away.

"He's lying," said Derek.

"About what."

"About today being Larry's birthday?"

"How do you know?"

"What date is today?"

"15th August."

"That's how I know it's not his birthday."

Harold looked at him perplexed and then at Bethany who had the same puzzled look on her face.

"He told us that the scorpion tattoo represented his birth sign, right, well, that's Scorpio," explained Derek. "The dates for Scorpio are 21 October to 20 November."

"How do you know about such things?" asked Harold.

"From Sheila, I told you how she was into spirituality, well, one if the things she went on about was the Zodiac, she was forever reciting the dates. It stuck with me."

"So, why would Jim lie?"

"I don't know but I intend to find out."

****

Harold lay on his bed, thinking. This was a strange place. Sheila had supposedly left but they had found her Chakra bracelet on a route Derek claimed they had never hiked before. Then Jim lied about it being Larry's birthday. Why would he lie? He had also asked him about a key. The key to this room maybe? He sat up and looked at the empty lock on the door. Most likely Sheila had taken it with her. Still, he looked around the room. He got up and opened the wardrobe, removing his clothes and searching the shelves. Nothing. She must have taken it with her. He went back to bed and closed his eyes.

****

He was awoken by a loud noise coming from below. He sat up and listened. A door closed on the ground floor. He swivelled onto the edge of the bed and placed his feet on the hard, wooden floor, Easing himself up he crept to his door as quietly as he could. Placing his hand gently on the handle he turned it slowly before pulling lightly. The door would not budge. He pulled more firmly but to no avail. The door was locked. He released the handle and staggered backwards stunned, he was locked in. Outside he could here muffled voices. He took the edge of the curtain and peeled it back so he could see through a thin slither. It was dark outside but he could just about make out three figures moving away from the barn towards the farmhouse until they disappeared. He got back into the bed. Unable to sleep he lay in his back and starred upwards, his mind racing. Why was his door locked? Who were those people outside? Stretton? Larry Dwyer? Thomas Buchanan? That was another thing, what was an educated professional like

Thomas Buchanan doing with roughnecks like Jim Stretton and Larry Dwyer? Suddenly he heard footsteps in the corridor. He held his breath as they grew louder. They were approaching his door. He sat up and stared wild eyed at the door, his heart beating fast in his chest. The footsteps stopped outside his door. He heard a key being inserted into the lock and turning. His eyes opened wider with fear. He could hear his own rapid breathing as he sat in the dark and deadly silence unable to move, paralysed with terror. The footsteps retreated down the hall. He fell back against the mattress, emitting a long sigh as his heart rate and breathing steadied. He resolved to leave this place.

****

Harold yawned and stretched his arms up to the clear blue sky. He looked up to the farmhouse. On the porch Thomas Buchanan was talking vigorously to Bethany. He was wagging his finger while she nodded earnestly. Suddenly, they stopped as they noticed Harold. Thomas gestured to Bethany and she descended the steps towards Harold. Thomas placed his hands on the porch fence and observed them closely.

"Morning, Harold," she greeted approaching.

"Morning, Bethany. What was all that about?"

"What?"

"He seemed to be scolding you."

"Oh, no, it was nothing."

Jim suddenly appeared.

"Right exercise time."

"Aren't you going to wait for Derek?"

"Derek is no longer here."

A look of astonishment came over his face.

"You mean he's left.?"

"Yea, that's right."

"When?"

"Last night."

He was about to say he was going to leave to and stopped himself. Why would Derek up and leave in the night?

∧∧∧∧∧∧∧∧∧∧

Thankfully the exercises finished early and Harold returned to his room before lunch. Exhausted he collapsed onto the bed causing one of the metal legs to rattle. He got up and knelt on the floor. Gripping the leg he shook it. From inside he could hear metallic rattling.

He tugged the mattress off and rested it against the wall before tilting the frame and positioning it on its side. Then gripping the rubber stopper on the foot of the leg he started to twist and pull. It was a little stiff but as he applied more force it began to move. Inch by inch it eased down until it finally came away. He tilted the frame forward and a metal object fell from the hollow leg, landing on the wooden floor with a jangle. The missing key.

Outside he could here men's voices. Quickly he replaced the bed, walked to the door and inserted the key carefully into the lock. He tried to turn it but it would not budge. Suddenly he heard footsteps coming up the stairs, he removed the key and slipped it into his pocket. He retreated to the bed and listened to the advancing steps. They stopped outside his door. He looked intensely at the door. There was a sudden knocking which made him jump. The handle began to turn, Harold held his breath as the door opened.

"Are you coming down to lunch?"

"Bethany! Sure I'll be down soon."

"What are you doing?"

"Nothing."

She surveyed the room, , Harold followed her gaze, the rubber stopper was still laying on the floor. He looked at her, scrutinising the object.

"Ok," she said finally. "See you in a bit."

Once she had gone Harold replaced the stopper on the leg and opened the wardrobe, taking out a pair of socks. He dropped the key into one of them, rolled it into a ball and placed it at the back of the wardrobe before heading downstairs.

****

It had been a quiet afternoon and Harold had returned to his room after dinner, He lay on the bed with his eyes open staring into the darkness. The key was clenched in his hand. It fitted into his lock so it was probable it opened a room in the barn. Why had Sheila hidden the key? Did she know what it opened?. Slowly he raised from the bed, slipping his phone into his pocket, the light would prove useful. He put one hand on the door handle and the other on the door, pressing it against the frame so it would not make a sound. The door opened inch by inch. It was pitch black in the corridor. He turned the light on his watch, crept stealthily to the next room and inserted the key. It refused to turn. He made his way down to the other rooms on the upper floor but the result was the same. There was no choice but to go down to the ground floor. He felt for the banister and made his way down. The stairs squeaked with each step he took. At the bottom he inserted the key into room 4, Derek's room. Nothing. Perhaps he was wrong and the key did not fit any of the rooms in the barn, He moved to room 3 and inserted the key. His heart rate increased, the key turned.

He stopped and stood back and looked nervously down the corridor before proceeding. With a trembling hand he turned the handle slowly. He could hear the sound of the mechanism in the door, amplified in the deathly dark. The door creaked open increasing his anxiety. He closed the door behind him and used the light on his phone to look around the room. Suitcases and holdalls were randomly scattered around the floor, some laying upside down, as though they had been carelessly thrown inside. Against the back wall was an old wooden bookshelf with a few plastic containers on the shelves. In the corner was a rusted metal filing cabinet. He stepped over the suitcases and approached the bookshelf. The containers were white with screw top lids. Harold removed one of the containers and shone the light on the label, "Weight Gain." He unscrewed the top and looked inside. The jar was half full of small white pills. He tilted the jar and emptied a few of the pills onto the shelf. They looked exactly the same as the ones he had been taking, supposedly for weight loss. Why would they be giving him weight gain tablets? He replaced the jar and stepped back tripping over something and crashing heavily to the floor. The noise was loud, he remained still and listened before shining the light on the object he had fallen over, It was the scales. He stared at the dial, the needle was set to minus ten pounds. Jim was giving them false readings, they were not losing weight at all, they were gaining it. He looked at all the suitcases, crawled to the nearest one and opened it. It was full of clothes. He pulled out a large pair of trousers and examined them. The waist was considerably larger than his own. He replaced them and moved onto the next case. Similarly full of clothes, this time dresses and skirts. Again with huge waistlines. It was the same with the next case and the next. He picked up a huge shirt and shone the light upon it illuminating dark red stains on the collar and down one sleeve. A chill went down his spine. He moved with increasing trepidation to the last case, undoing the clasps and lifting the lid. Woman's clothes, large clothing like all the others. He reached inside and his hand felt something hard below the clothes. His fingers closed around it. He held it up to the light. The gemstones sparkled, red, yellow and purple in the tail and green and blue in the wings. The Chakra dragonfly necklace. Sheila. He shoved it into his pocket and shone the light back around the room. The beam stopped on the filing cabinet. He stepped over the cases towards it, turned the handle pulled. The rust had caused it to seize. He put the light on the floor and placed both hands on the handle. As he tugged it opened with a creaking jerky action. He picked up the light and shone it inside illuminating the shelf. Harold recoiled, covering his mouth in horror. On the centre of the shelf with the eyes and mouth open was the bloodied, severed head of Derek. He closed the door and staggered back repulsed, his mind in a daze. Suddenly he felt a hand on his shoulder. He spun round.

"Bethany!"

"What are you doing in here?"

"We have to get out of this place."

"What do you mean?"

"Did you see what was inside the cabinet?"

"No. What?"

"Just as well," he said gripping her hand and dragging her from the room.

"Where are you taking me?" protested Bethany, struggling to loosen his grip as they stepped out of the building and into the cold night air.

"They're killers."

"Who?"

"All of therm."

"Help!" she shouted.

"Stay quiet, you'll wake them."

A light went on in the farmhouse.

"Run," screamed Harold as Bethany broke free, reeling backwards and fell to the ground.

Harold looked down at her in desperation then saw the figures on the porch. He ran towards the road. Behind him he could hear them running after him and saw the torches shinning all around him. He got off the road and onto the hiking trail. His pursuers were getting closer. He scrambled up frantically over the uneven terrain, his foot slipped and he fell to the ground clutching his ankle and groaning. The voices and lights were getting nearer, he struggle to his feet, hobbled forward a few steps and collapsed. It was no use, he turned his head and shone his light on his pursuers, illuminating the faces of Jim, Larry, Thomas and Mary.

"I know everything," he screamed. "I've been in room 3."

You shouldn't have done that, Harold," said Jim menacingly.

"I found the pills to make us gain weight you passed off as slimming tablets,"

The four drew nearer through the darkness, their beams all focused on Harold, lying helpless on the ground.

"And the scales, rigged to make us believe we were losing weight when we were getting heavier."

He tried to clamber up the slope dragging his swollen ankle behind him as the group moved with a sinister slowness towards him.

"I know how you all know each other. I thought it was strange when Larry said he would never fly again, he was on the plane that crashed in the Andes, you all were. Five survivors who managed to stay alive for two whole months. How? All the evidence is in room 3, the belongings of all the victims. I bet Sheila knew, she had the key, she saw, that's why she tried to escape. I know what you are."

"And what's that, Harold?" asked Jim smiling maliciously.

"Cannibals. You survived in the Andes by eating the dead passengers."

"They weren't all dead, at the beginning," said Jim as the group surrounded him and hovered ominously over him.

"You're beasts," yelled Harold defiantly.

"We did what we had to do to survive," said Thomas calmly. "One develops a taste for the exquisite. You cannot imagine the succulence of human flesh."

"You're animals."

"How many survivors were there, Harold?" asked Thomas.

"Five."

"That's right."

The group parted and Harold saw the fifth member approaching, light glistening off the jagged blade in Bethany's hand. Harold slumped back resigned to his fate.

LORRY

"The search is still continuing for Tina Reynolds, the 22 year old student who went missing in Edinburgh last week. If anyone has any information please contact Police Scotland on..."

The trucker reached forward and changed the channel.

♫ *"...Get your motor runnin'*

Head out on the highway

Lookin' for adventure

In whatever comes our way..."♫

The music boomed around the cabin over the roar of the engine and the noise of the tyres on the tarmac. The array of headlights shone through the darkness illuminating the desolate surroundings, the bare trees and remnants of snow in clumps below, as the lorry rumbled along the winding road. Inside, the portly trucker tapped his gloved fingers on the wheel to the beat of the music.

♫ *"...Born to be wild*

Born to be wild..."♫

He pulled up the zip on his donkey jacket, adjusted his baseball cap and turned up the heater causing the newspaper on the dashboard to lightly flutter. The full moon shone and stars

107

twinkled above in the clear night sky, the snow on the side of the road getting higher as the lorry began to ascend. As it went over the brow of the hill and descended the headlights dipped onto something at the side. The trucker widened his eyes incredulously, it was a man, stood with his thumb out. A hitchhiker at this time of night and in the middle of winter? He deserves a lift if for no other reason than to hear his story, he thought. The lorry shuddered to a halt. The engine hummed as the trucker turned on the inner light and waited patiently with intrigue. A few seconds later the passenger door opened revealing a scrawny individual with long, dirty hair and stubbled chin wearing a faded, camouflage jacket and torn denim jeans with a large, canvas rucksack on his back.

"Where are you going?" asked the trucker.

"Inverness."

"I can take you as far as Aviemore."

He nodded and lifted his rucksack into the cabin, scrambling up behind it.

"Thanks for stopping, it's freezing out there, you're the first vehicle I have seen."

"What have you got in there?" asked the trucker looking at the bulging bag.

"Just my things."

He closed the door causing the rucksack to topple against the trucker.

"Better put that in the back," he said disgruntled.

"Ah, ok."

The hitcher got back out, dragging the rucksack down behind him, it hit the ground with a thud. The trucker watched as he struggled to lift it onto his back wondering what on earth he had in there that was so heavy. The hitcher went to the rear of the lorry and put his hand onto the rusted handle, immediately letting go before his skin stuck to the icy metal. He worked the sleeve of his jacket over his palm, gripped it firmly and pulled. It refused to budge, stuck solid by the cold and rust. He put both hands on the handle, tightened his grip and tugged with all his might causing it to screech and move a fraction. He yanked it repeatedly, inching it open, sweat forming on his forehead with his exertions. Finally he was able to swing the door open. He peered inside, although it was dark he could see it was empty save for a large sheet of tarpaulin bundled up in the far corner. He lifted his rucksack in,

The trucker listened to the metallic creaking as the rear door closed. The hitcher reappeared and climbed into the cabin. He was panting and dishevelled and for the first time the trucker noticed his wild, piercing eyes. The hitcher leant forward and looked at the front-page headline on the newspaper.

POLICE CONTINUE SEARCH

FOR TINA REYNOLDS

Below it was a photograph of a young, fresh faced woman with long blonde hair. The trucker turned out the light and the lorry continued on its way.

"Why are you going to Inverness at this time of night?" asked the trucker.

"I had to get out of Edinburgh."

"At this time of night?"

"When I decide to do something I do it."

The trucker fell silent, the lorry wound its way around the country roads.

"What are you picking up in Aviemore?" asked the hitcher.

"What makes you think I'm picking something up?"

"You're not delivering anything, it was dark back there but apart from a sheet of tarpaulin on the floor your container is empty."

The trucker paused.

"Is it a secret?"

"Whisky," he said finally.

"Oh-ho, I'm partial to a wee malt myself. Which one?"

"Famous Grouse."

"Ah, a blended, not as good. Do you get a free bottle or two?"

"No."

"Pity, I didn't even know there was a distillery in Aviemore."

The trucker remained silent with his eyes on the road. As the lorry rolled around a bend the newspaper fell to the floor at the hitcher's feet. He bent forward and retrieved it.

"She's dead," he said replacing it on the dashboard.

"Who?"

"That woman who went missing last week, Tina Reynolds. That's usually the way when someone goes missing, her body will probably be discovered buried under the floorboards. That's the trouble with killing someone, what do you do with the body?"

"I suppose."

"I would bury it somewhere remote, like the woods."

"What about all the animals foraging around? They would soon locate a decomposing corpse."

"You would need to bury it deep, six feet. That would also stop the police sniffer dogs detecting the scent."

"I don't know, those sniffer dogs are quite adept at finding bodies."

The hitcher furrowed his brow in concentration.

"I know, bury the body at ten feet and put a dead animal at six feet, then when the grave is dug up the police would think the dogs had detected the animal scent. It wouldn't occur to them to dig below."

"That's a lot of digging. It's hard to dig ten feet, especially at night in the cold and the dark."

"Dig the hole in advance in the daytime."

"You take the risk of being seen during the day."

"Then use a grave that has already been dug."

"Where are you going to find that?"

"A cemetery, of course. You would have to use one where a coffin had just been buried so the earth would be loose and easy to move. Then put your body under the coffin. The beauty of a graveyard is the police would never take the dogs in, too many dead bodies, it would be like taking a metal detector into a nail factory."

The hitcher chortled at his own joke.

"It takes four people to even carry a coffin, how are you going to manage to lift it?"

"You spoil all my ideas," bemoaned the hitcher, abruptly ceasing his laughter. "Ok. Forget the burial. How about dissolving he body? Yes, dissolve it in a bath of hydrochloric acid."

"Have you ever used hydrochloric acid to dispose of something? It absolutely stinks, plus it will not dissolve bones."

"It's the bones that are the biggest problem, The only way I can think of is to burn them in a furnace of some sort, a funeral director would make the perfect serial killer with his access to cremation."

"What if you don't have access to a crematorium?"

"Then I guess you're back to burying it, I still think this is the best idea. If you find a remote location I don't think it would be discovered."

"Like here in the highland wilderness?"

"Perfect."

"How would you move the body, a heavy thing, a dead body?"

"Cut it up and put in in a sack."

"Gruesome work."

"I saw worse in Afghanistan?"

"You are in the army?"

"I was, I saw sights that effect the balance of your mind."

The hitcher looked blankly at the road ahead, his jaw clenched and face hardened. The truck moved through the darkness as the next song played on the radio.

♫ *"...The silicon chip inside her head*

Gets switched to overload

And nobody's gonna go to school today

She's gonna make them stay at home..."♫

The lorry continued along the winding road, the trees getting denser on each side. From a layby the young officer watched from the patrol car as the vehicle roared past. The driver's door opened.

"What's it like out there, sarge?"

"Bloody cold," replied the sergeant quickly getting in. "That's better, I was bursting. What was that I heard?

113

"A lorry."

"Unusual to get a lorry on this road. I wonder where he's going at this time of night. Did you see any company name on it."

"No, no markings, at all."

"That's strange, I think we'll follow it, take a look."

"Hang on I have to go now too," said the young officer opening his door.

"Hurry up then. Billy"

The truck sped around the country roads, the music filling the cabin.

♫ *"...And he can see no reasons*

'Cause there are no reasons

What reason do you need to die..."♫

The hitcher spoke slowly and deliberately.

"I used to drive a truck like this along the Kabul-Kandahar Road."

"You should get back into it, there's a shortage of drivers right now."

" I can't."

114

"Sure you can."

"I told you I can't," he hissed.

The men fell silent again.

"And now for the news. Clothes believed to belong to missing student Tina Reynold's have been found in a derelict house on the outskirts of Edinburgh."

"Told you, dead."

"Not necessarily."

"What do you think then, she's walking around the streets of Edinburgh naked? mocked the hitcher laughing derisively. "Maybe that's who those cops are looking for."

"What cops?"

"We passed a patrol car a few minutes ago."

"I didn't see it."

"It was parked in the layby with its lights off but I could see the outline of the sirens on the roof."

The lorry pulled in and stopped.

"What are you doing?" asked the hitcher surprised as the trucker turned on the light.

"Sorting you out."

He stared at the hitcher, studying his increasingly tense face, the vein above his right eye beginning to throb.

"Take the wheel,," he ordered opening his door and disembarking. "Once a trucker, always a trucker."

The hitcher glared at the multi coloured dials on the instrument panel, the levers, the pedals and finally the big round steering wheel. His door opened sharply.

"What are you waiting for? Move over."

The hitcher unclipped his belt and tentatively sidled across into the driver's seat. He moved his hands slowly towards the steering wheel and gripped it until his knuckles went white. The trucker looked at the hitcher and for the first time noticed that his jeans were splattered with dark red stains. He clambered up and closed the door. The light extinguished and they sat silently in the darkness. The hitcher stared blankly at the wheel, in his head he was back on the Kabul-Kandahar Road surrounded by flashes and explosions. The captain shouting and a fellow shoulder screaming as a bullet ripped through his body, watching as he fell bleeding to the dusty ground. He gritted his teeth, put the lorry into gear, released the brake and pressed the accelerator. He felt the power as the lorry moved off.

"What happened to your jeans?"

"What do you mean?" replied the hitcher defensively.

"They are all ripped up."

"They're old."

"What about those stains?"

"I don't know."

"It looks like blood."

The hitcher's vein pulsated more intensely as he ground his teeth together.

"I fell and cut my legs."

"When?"

"A few days ago, what is this an interrogation?"

The hitcher gripped the gear stick and rammed it violently into a lower gear as the truck ascended a small hill. The trucker looked at him sceptically, before focusing on the road ahead, why didn't he change his clothes? He thought about the newspaper headline:

POLICE CONTINUE SEARCH

FOR TINA REYNOLDS

"Where were you before here?"

"I told you that already, Edinburgh."

"What did you do there?"

"What do you mean?"

"Do you work?"

"I don't have a job anymore."

"Why don't you go back to trucking?"

"Look, I've got a criminal record, alright."

"What for?"

"It was a long time ago, I don't want to talk about it."

The trucker's mind raced.

"Pull in, I think I can hear the rear doors open."

"I can't hear anything, I secured them when I put my rucksack in."

"Better stop and I'll do a quick check."

The lorry slowed and stopped. The trucker climbed down from the cabin and disappeared from view. The hitcher took his hands from the wheel and wiped his forehead. He picked up the newspaper and read the article on the missing woman. She was dead, he knew it, the police would never find out who did it. So, they had found her clothes but they would never find the body. The police always think they are so smart. What was taking that trucker so long, he thought, clenching and unclenching his hands on the wheel. He glanced into the side mirror, he could see the container door swung open but no sign of the trucker. Where the hell was he? In the distance he observed the headlights of an approaching vehicle. His eyes narrowed as it got closer and closer until he could see its outline, the patrol car. It pulled in behind the lorry. The hitcher watched suspiciously as the door opened and a large, uniformed officer stepped out. His sight never faltered as the policeman walked slowly and decisively along the side of the truck until he appeared at the window. The hitcher studied his bearded face and noted the three stripes on his sleeve. He wound down the window.

"Can I ask where you are going, sir?"

"Aviemore, the distillery."

"There's no distillery in Aviemore. Please step down, sir."

The hitcher observed a second officer at the front running a check on the registration plate. He descended from the cabin. The sergeant immediately noticed the dark red stains on his torn jeans

"What's your name?"

"I'm just hitching."

"Name!"

"Thomas McLean, but I'm not the driver."

"You're the only one here."

"The trucker got out to check the rear doors."

The younger officer emerged at the window.

"I ran a check on the registration plate, this vehicle was reported stolen earlier this evening."

"Where did you steal the lorry from?" demanded the sergeant.

"I don't know anything about any stolen lorry, I hitched a lift about half an hour ago."

"Billy, check the name, Thomas McLean, So, you weren't driving?"

"No."

"But you were in the driver's seat?"

"I took the wheel for a few minutes, that's all. Ask the trucker," he implored looking frantically about.

"There's nobody else here."

"Look, I'm telling you, I was hitching, I got picked up about ten miles back. The trucker is around here somewhere, big burly guy wearing a donkey jacket and baseball cap."

"So, someone else was driving/"

"Yes."

"That's easily proved we'll dust the wheel for fingerprints."

"No, he was wearing gloves."

The sergeant looked at him with increasing disbelief.

"Look, I'm telling you the truth."

The hitcher was becoming more agitated with each passing second.

"Thomas McLean, banned from driving," stated the young officer reading from his screen.

The hitcher's mind raced.

"Let's take a look in the back,"

"Ah, my rucksack, that will prove I'm a hitcher."

The three men moved to the back.

"Why are the doors open?" enquired the sergeant with increasing suspicion.

"The trucker opened them, he said they were not closed properly."

He scrutinised the hitcher before removing a torch from his pocket and shining it inside. The beam probed the container, empty except for the sheet of tarpaulin bundled up on the floor at the back.

"My rucksack, it's gone, it was right here at the front," said the hitcher frantically. "He's taken it."

He began to scramble up but a firm hand on his shoulder dragged him back.

"We'll examine it if you don't mind. Billy, take a look"

The young officer climbed up into the container and began rooting around. His torch beam scoured the floor.

"Nothing up here, sarge"

"What's under the tarpaulin?"

The young officer shone his torch on the large bundle against the back wall and made his way carefully through the dusty container. He knelt down and pulled the top. It was heavier than it looked. He placed the torch on the floor and using both hands began to unravel the heavy material while the hitcher watched him with growing angst. The tarpaulin obscured his view as Billy picked up the torch and shone it in behind.

"Sarge, you'd better get up here."

He clambered up. The hitcher looked at the backs of the policemen bent over the tarpaulin straining to see what it was. He could hear the two officers whispering but it was too quiet

121

to understand the words. They both stopped and looked at the hitcher then walked towards him and descended. They closed the doors in silence before facing him. The sergeant spoke firmly and clearly as he removed the handcuffs from his belt.

"Thomas McLean, I am arresting you for the murder of Tina Reynolds."

MAGIC

AUTHOR'S INTRODUCTION

Long regarded as the most dangerous and daring illusion in magic is the bullet catch, where a gun is fired directly at the magician who attempts to catch it in his mouth. It is believed to have first been performed by the French magician Couleu in 1581. Since then it has been performed by many, using various techniques to make it safer, but the deadly risk still remains. In fact, over 12 magicians have been killed while performing the feat.

In this tale Jonathan is a struggling sculptor who makes magic props for the Great Contini to supplement his meagre income and keep the debt collector from his door. The two men share more than just a business relationship and as the situation become increasingly difficult he is compelled to take drastic action.

"I will now perform the famous bullet catch," announced the magician to the expectant audience.

Behind him a large sign was emblazoned in bright red letters with the name THE GREAT CONTINI. He stood magnificently, the lights illuminating the crisp white shirt below his dark navy jacket. Despite his jet black hair and moustache the lines on his face were showing his age. He was flanked by an alluring young assistant dressed in high heeled boots.

"The bullet will be fired from this rifle held by my beautiful assistant, Bianca" he continued gesturing dramatically to the gun. Bianca's perfect white teeth gleamed as she smiled radiantly, displaying the weapon to the crowd.

"Bianca, the bullets, please."

She tossed back her long, blonde hair and took a small velvet covered box from the table. She opened the lid slowly to reveal six shining bullets, showing the audience before giving them to Contini. He selected one of the bullets and loaded it into the gun. At the far end of the stage was positioned a rectangular target on a stand depicting the outline of a man's head and torso. He raised the rifle to his cheek and took aim. The shot rang out around the theatre as he pulled the trigger, a single hole was visible in the centre of the head.

"The bullet to be fired will be chosen by a member of the audience," he declared lowering the weapon.

Bianca scanned the faces of the spectators before descending the stairs and offering the bullets to an old man. He looked at the gleaming bullets, hovered his hand over the box

125

and picked up one from the centre. Bianca took it from him, returned to the stage and handed it to the magician.

"I will now cut a cross on the bullet."

He took a small knife from his pocket and carved an "X" on the tip.

"I will attempt to catch this bullet between my teeth," he said. "For this I will require complete silence. Many magicians have been killed attempting this feat."

He cocked back the rifle, opened the chamber, inserted the bullet and placed it on top of the table. The theatre was hushed in anticipation. He moved across the stage and stood with the back of his head perfectly aligned with that drawn on the target.

"The bullet will be fired through a pane of glass."

Bianca glided to the back of the stage and wheeled out a rectangular pane of glass on a metal stand. The audience was so hushed the clacking of her stiletto heels cold be heard on the wooden stage floor as she moved elegantly. She positioned the glass directly between Contini and the rifle before moving behind the table. The audience was captivated as she picked up the gun slowly and deliberately, placing the butt against her cheek and taking careful aim. She positioned her finger on the trigger. The audience held its collective breath. She squeezed the trigger, the bullet exploded from the barrel as the glass shattered sending shards flying to the ground. Contini fell back against the target as audible gasps could be heard from the crowd. He staggered upright, reached into his mouth and held the bullet triumphantly aloft, displaying the carved cross to an applauding audience.

****

Contini sat at the table, the lights surrounding the mirror before him illuminating a hipflask and a wad of notes. He bent over the pile, thumbing through them as he counted.

"It's all there," said a slim man in a suit and thin tie hanging limply from an open collared shirt.

"I want a bigger cut, Donald."

"That is the amount we agreed."

Contini unscrewed the hipflask and took a swig.

"If this is not doubled, I walk, " he said shaking the bundle. "There are plenty of other venues in this city who would love to host the act."

Donald clenched his jaw tight and curled his hands into fists behind his back.

"Just go," barked Contini taking another slug from the hipflask.

"One day, you will go too far, Contini."

He turned abruptly and stormed across the room, grabbing the door knob violently and hurling it open coming face to face with Bianca. He glared at her.

"You can do better than him," he hissed as he stomped passed her.

Bianca watched him disappear with a stunned look on her face.

"Bring that cute little body over here," slurred Contini taking yet another swig from the flask.

"Wait until I have shut the door," she replied closing it hastily.

As she approached him he lunged forward, grabbed her around her exposed waist and pulled her onto his lap, kissing her ruby red lips before moving onto her bare neck. She placed her hands on his chest and pushed herself back.

"I want more than this," she said firmly.

"Oh, you'll get more than this," he replied with a mischievous glint in his eye, trying to pull her towards him but her outstretched arms locked on his chest resisting.

"You know what I mean."

"What would you have me do?"

"Leave her."

"I will."

"When?"

"When the time is right."

"You always say that. It's me or her, I mean it."

"You know I want to be with you, just give me a bit more time."

She looked into his eyes trying to read his true feelings.

"Melissa means nothing to me," he reassured her. "You know you're the only one now."

She softened her arms and kissed his lips tenderly

"What's this?" he asked.

She sat back and he reached behind her long golden earring and flamboyantly produced a condom.

****

The woman opened her eyes slowly focusing on the cracks on the ceiling above, She stretched out her naked body, gripping the metal headboard and yawning as she extended her long legs and curled her toes. Below she could hear metal banging. She slipped from the bed and appraised her body in the full length mirror, her breasts were not as pert as they once were and the lines on her face were getting more pronounced. She brushed her thick auburn hair down with her hands, at least there was no grey, yet. Below the banging was replaced by heavy footsteps pacing up and down on the wooden floor. She wrapped a robe around her body and peered over the balcony onto the lower level. The young man paced up and down, stopping occasionally, looking at the block of stone on the table with the beginnings of a face carved. He shook his head and ran his hand feverishly through his hair, tugging the strands over his shoulder. The woman descended the open spiral stairwell from the mezzanine level silently, she knew better than to speak when he was like this. He stood as though transfixed, looking at the stone. Suddenly he moved forwards, grabbed the chisel, placed it on the stone and started to tap the end with a small hammer. Small chips fell on the table. He stepped back, scrutinising his work before chiselling again. As he hammered the chisel more firmly a large chunk of stone fragmented and landed with a thud. The sculptor looked at it wild eyed.

"It's ruined!" he yelled.

He hurled the chisel violently across the studio, hitting an easel and knocking it over with a resounding crash.

"This stone is rubbish, how can I be expected to work with it," be bemoaned slumping back in the chair.

The woman looked around the studio at the half finished sculptures and incomplete paintings, some on easels, some lying torn on the dusty floor. She approached the small fridge at the rear of the studio and opened the door. The inside was grimy and empty bar for a small amount of milk in a container. She picked it up, unscrewed the lid and sniffed it pulling it quickly from her nose and reading the label.

"This milk expired three days ago, Jonathan."

She put it back and picked up the letter lying on top of the fridge. The words FINAL DEMAND were printed in bold red letters across the top. Below was the account details.

"Jonathan you haven't paid the rent on this place for the past six months?"

He slumped on top of the table and buried his face in his arms. She approached and looked at him lying in the dust covered top, stones scattered about him. In the centre of the table was a bullet and behind it exact replicas made of wax. She picked up the live round and examined it. He looked up lazily.

"It's a sad state of affairs, I earn more from making wax bullets for Contini than any of my art," he said ruefully.

"Can you help me out?"

"You know I can't, Jonathan. He keeps a tight rein on finances."

She wrapped her hand around the bullet made a dramatic gesture in the air, opened her palm and it was gone.

"Very funny, Melissa, give it back?"

She reached inside her robe and produced the bullet.

"Pretty good, don't you think?"

"Great," he mumbled wearily.

"I can still do all the tricks of "the Great Contini"," she said placing the bullet down.

"All of them?"

"All of them, I was a magician in my own right before I met him but he made me give it all up."

"Why don't you leave him?"

"We have been over this, Jonathan, if I leave I get nothing, he has an iron clad prenup contract."

He picked up the bullet and twirled it in his fingers, looking at it intensely.

"Perhaps there is another way."

****

The old car spluttered to a halt outside the theatre. The rusted door opened with a creak and Jonathan stepped out.

"Bloody hell, the last time I saw something like that it was in a museum," commented Donald leaning on the open stage door.

"It gets me about," said Jonathan ambling towards him while he pulled his shabby coat down.

"What does he want to see you about?"

"Probably more bullets for the act."

"Pity you can't make a real one, do us all a favour."

Jonathan smiled weakly and followed him down the narrow, dimly lit corridor.

"He's waiting for you inside," said Donald nodding to a door at the end of the passage.

Jonathan continued alone and knocked on the door.

"Come!"

In the office Contini sat behind a small desk shrouded in smoke from a cigar hanging from the side of his mouth. Around the room were the magic act props, a long rectangular box with a saw on top, a deck of oversized cards and in front of him a black top hat and a wand. In the corner Jonathan observed the rifle.

"I need new bullets, something that will make a bigger, more dramatic explosion when it hits the glass," demanded Contini.

"I'll try a different type of wax."

"Have it ready for the show tomorrow night."

"That might be a bit soon."

"Have it by tomorrow or I will get somebody else to make them."

"I'll see what I can do."

"That's all." he said dismissively waving Jonathan away with his hand.

Jonathan arrived back at his studio to find a familiar car waiting outside. As he approached the front door two man got out of the car. He looked at them anxiously. The driver was a big burly man with a shaved head wearing a tan leather jacket. The other was slim and well dressed in a suit and tie, the elegant clothes masking his sinister intentions.

"We have been waiting for you, Jonathan."

"I'll have the money soon, Paul, I just need a bit more time."

"You have had more than enough time. Let's discuss it inside."

Jonathan opened the studio and the men followed him in, the burly one closing and locking the door behind him.

"The money, Jonathan, We have been very patient with you."

"I have money coming, I swear, just give me a few more days."

Paul picked up a thin chisel and ran his finger along the sharp tip.

"It will be very difficult for you to sculpt without fingers, I think."

Jonathan watched him as he placed the tip on top of a sculpted head. He picked up the hammer and with one mighty blow embedded the chisel into the skull.

"Very well, one more week, after that we shall start removing fingers."

The two men left, Jonathan listened as the car drove off. He bolted the door and moved to the table. Before him was the bullet and a lump of wax. He picked up the wax and began to melt it with his lighter until it dripped into a saucer below. Slowly, drop by drop the saucer began to fill. He put the wax down and picked up the bullet. Carefully he dipped the tip into the hot wax, then took a small brush and meticulously smoothed it evenly around the bullet. He stood it upright on the table and left it to harden.

****

Jonathan stood in the backstage corridor and looked at the box in his hand. He opened the lid, inside was the wax covered bullet. Contini would certainly inspect it. It was good, Jonathan knew it was good, it looked exactly like the others he had made, it had to be. He closed the lid, took a deep breath and knocked on the door.

"Come!"

Inside the blinds were closed making the room dimmer than usual.

"Do you have it?" asked Contini.

Jonathan put the box down on the desk. Contini opened it and looked at the bullet. Jonathan watched him intensely as he removed the bullet, lifted it to his eye and examined it carefully. He rotated the bullet then ran his finger over the wax, pursing his lips. Jonathan felt the perspiration on his forehead. Contini placed it flat on his palm and moved his hand up and down as though he was assessing the weight. He placed it back in the box, reclined in his chair and pressed his fingertips together as he scrutinised Jonathan. Jonathan tried to read his thoughts, had he identified the bullet as being real, had he felt the wax covering? Had he felt a change in weight?

"Why is their only one?"

"It's to try, if you like it I can make more."

"It feels different to the others."

"I used a different wax?"

Jonathan held his breath.

"Very well, I'll use it in tonight's show."

135

****

Contini sat in the restaurant with Melissa.

"Tonight will be a special show, Melissa."

"Uh-huh," she replied from behind the menu.

The waiter appeared at the table.

"Are you ready to order?"

"You order, Melissa, I'm still deciding."

"I will take the salmon, please,"

Contini studied the menu while the waiter stood patiently.

"Just have your usual blue steak," said Melissa testily.

"No, I think I'll have the mussels."

"Mussels? You remember what happened last time you had mussels."

"Yes, definitely the mussels."

He placed the menu down and smiled.

Jonathan had been texting and ringing Melissa's phone all afternoon but she had not answered. He paced up and down the studio, glancing intermittently at his watch with increasing tension in his face. He peered through the window into the darkness, taking out his phone one more time and pressing it to his ear, listening intensely. *"You have reached the phone of*

136

Melissa Contini, please leave a..." He hit the cancel button, grabbed his car keys and left the studio.

The magician fired the rifle into the target, the explosion making the audience gasp. Bianca descended the stairs in front of the stage with the velvet box and offered the bullets to an old lady in the front row. She looked at the row of bullets apprehensively. Bianca smiled encouragingly, a frail hand reached into the box and picked up a bullet. Bianca took it from her, returned to the stage and handed it to the magician. A cross was carved into the tip of the bullet and held up to the audience. The rifle chamber was opened and with a quick sleight of hand the magician palmed the bullet and inserted the new wax one before moving assuredly across the stage and standing in front of the target. While the audience were distracted watching the pane of glass being wheeled out the magician deftly slipped the carved bullet into the mouth. Bianca lifted the gun to her cheek and took aim.

Jonathan parked at the rear of the theatre and entered through the stage door. He moved quickly along the dimly lit passage towards the back of the stage, his heart was beating fast. Suddenly he stopped and listened, it was eerily quiet. He looked furtively at his watch, the act should be over now, had something gone wrong? A dark silhouette appeared at the end of the corridor. Donald? The figure raised a hand and beckoned to him. Jonathan moved cautiously forwards, the light from the stage making him increasingly more visible. No, how can this be, Contini.

137

"Has the act finished?" asked Jonathan, attempting to cover the tremor in his voice.

"No."

Jonathan looked at him perplexed.

"Did you really think I wouldn't recognise the bullet covered in wax?" said Contini.

Jonathan remained silent.

"At first I was going to inform the police but then I had a better idea. She never got your messages," said Contini producing Melissa's phone. "I have known about you two for a long time. Divorce is so messy, this is much better."

"Where is Melissa? he asked with increasing desperation.

"Did she ever tell you the story of how I got food poisoning from eating mussels? Another magician had to step in and do the show that night. I had mussels today, it was very easy to mimic the symptoms."

"Where is Melissa?" repeated Jonathan, his eyes widening and his mouth dry as the terrible truth began to dawn on him.

"See for yourself."

Contini stood aside. Jonathan moved passed him until he could see Bianca standing with the rifle raised. He looked down the stage to the far end in horror at the magician standing before the target, Melissa.

The shot and the screams rang out around the theatre.

HAUNTED

Mike looked at the dust covered sign on the lift, "OUT OF ORDER," and sighed heavily with his shoulders slumped. He turned and trudged up the stairs, his coat hanging loosely in his hand, dragging over each step picking up specks of dirt. After six flights he arrived at a paint, flaked door and inserted a key into the increasingly rusted lock. The door squeaked open and he pressed the switch on the wall. The light above flickered, then died. He toggled the switch up and down, it flickered to life again, brightly illuminated the sitting room and the brown envelope laying at his feet before fading to a dim glow. He ran his hand through his hair, tugging at the last few strands before bending down and picking it up.

"Bella!"

He tossed his jacket onto the sagging sofa, landing beside the torn cushion and went immediately to the small table, picked up the half full bottle of whisky and poured a large quantity into the waiting glass before seizing it up to his lips and emptying the contents into his mouth. He tore the envelope open and unfolded the letter. At the top in bold, black letters was the name Foster & Wyatt Solicitors. He quickly scanned the paragraph below, "overdue rent arrears."

"Bella!"

He screwed the paper into a ball and dropped it on the floor before refilling the glass and going into the kitchen. The sink was full of crockery protruding at varying angles, a pot encrusted with the remains of vegetable soup was perched precariously on top. He groaned looking at the teetering pile and took another swig from the glass.

"BELLA!"

He returned to the sitting room, a cool breeze fluttered the curtains partially covering the open window.

"Are you hiding from me?"

He crossed the room, pulled back the curtain and looked out into the darkness.

"Ah, there you are. What are you doing out there?"

He drank the remains of the whisky, put the glass down. opened the adjacent door and moved along the balcony to the metal fire escape staircase. The steel creaked as he descended and he placed his hand on the banister. Suddenly, the step beneath his foot gave way sending a piece of metal crashing to the ground below and causing him to stumble forwards over the side. His head lurched downwards, he gripped the banister tight and managed to stop himself plunging to his death. Gasping for breath, he stared at the concrete far below. He pushed himself back and slumped onto the steps, wiping the sweat from his forehead as he regained his composure. Bella climbed onto his lap and purred.

"You're nothing but trouble."

He stroked its sleek black fur. By the light from the sitting room he could just about see the hole in the step. He stood up with Bella in his arms and went back inside. The cat jumped from his arms and sat on the worn rug watching him close the window and draw the curtains. Her ears pricked up as a sudden buzzing emanated from the sofa. Mike's head drooped onto his chest, Bella leapt onto the sofa and started tugging at his jacket with her claws. Mike lumbered forwards and removed the vibrating mobile from his jacket pocket. His grip tightened as he read the message.

142

Trevor: You were late with deliveries again today. Come in one hour earlier tomorrow. I'll be here at 6.

He hurled it violently onto the sofa, causing Bella to jump quickly down as it bounced off the cushion and landed on the floor. She followed Mike to the table and rubbed her warm body against his leg while he poured another drink. He returned to the sofa, slumping down and looking blankly at the phone on the ground. Finishing the whisky he lay back and closed his eyes. Bella climbed on top of him and placed her head on his stomach he was already lightly snoring.

It was still dark as he got into his car and out of the cold, icy morning air.

"Come on, come on."

He turned the key repeatedly in the ignition with no response from the engine. A quick glance at his watch, 5.30am. He turned the key again and again, feeling the perspiration already on the back of his shirt. The engine spluttered and died.

"No, no, no, no, no."

He twisted the key violently and pumped the accelerator. The engine screamed, he released the handbrake and with the wheels screeching against the tarmac the car shot down the road.

Mike pulled up alongside a row of cars lined up outside the huge warehouse. He got out and looked at the drivers putting boxes into their vehicles as quickly as they could.

"6:04. I'm marking you down as late, one more demerit and you're out."

The portly man in a shirt and tie made a mark on his clipboard.

"Right this is yours," he said gesturing to a large pile of boxes.

Mike looked open eyed at the stack.

"They are not all going to fit in my car, Trevor."

"Then you will have to make two trips, won't you."

Mike looked into his grinning face.

"This is twice as much as usual."

"Harry Smith has been sacked, too many demerits, so you will have to take his today as well as your own."

Demerits for being late, demerits for being off sick, demerits for late deliveries, Mike had seen a lot of good people come and go.

"Are you just going to look at those boxes all day, time is money, they all need to be delivered today."

Mike opened his boot and started loading the boxes. This is what he had been reduced to since the car plant closed, no longer a skilled worker but just a cog in the over hyped gig economy where peeing in a bottle was de rigour. He opened the rear doors and stacked boxes on the floor and back seat until they were so high they obscured the windows. Still a few packages remained in the yard. There was no way he was making two trips. He opened the passenger door and placed

144

boxes on the floor and seat, even managing to cram a couple into the glove compartment and a long slim box between the seats so he was only just able to reach the handbrake.

The streets were fairly quiet as the sun began to rise. Mike looked at the boxes surrounding him, this was going to be a long shift. His phone bleeped from the dashboard holder.

Trevor: Have you made your first delivery?

Mike: Not yet.

Trevor: Get a move on.

Mike increased the pressure on the accelerator.

It was like groundhog day. Day after day, driving from house to house, and flat to flat. He should have studied harder in school, got into a profession that would stand the test of time. Manufacturing was all but dead, he might as well be a fletcher or a blacksmith.

He stopped outside a small bungalow, got out, opened the boot and looked at all the boxes. Mrs, Jones, it could be any of them. He picked up the top box and smiled broadly, Mrs. Jones. It was like winning the lottery if you found the box first time. He hurried to the door and rang the bell. No reply. He rang again. He did not want to make a second visit this far away from the other deliveries. He went around the back. There was a neatly mown lawn with a small greenhouse. He opened the door and slipped the parcel inside writing a note as he returned to the front and slipping it through the letterbox.

Back in the car his phone had another message.

Trevor: Have you made your first delivery yet?

Mike: Just done it.

He hit the accelerator and the wheels spun as he shot off down the road.

A couple of hours later the traffic was getting heavier as more and more people made their way to work. He turned off the main road into an area of small apartment blocks. Stopping by the kerb he got out and opened the boot, searching the boxes in vain for Mr. Kinross. He went to the back seat and rifled through the packages.

"Where the hell is it?"

He started piling boxes up on the pavement until only one small box remained.

"Typical, the last one."

He stuffed the other packages back in and slammed the door before walking briskly to the apartment block and pressing the buzzer. No response. He rammed his finger onto the button and held it down. Nothing. He pressed the other buttons, tapping his foot on the floor impatiently, was nobody in the block?

"Yea," barked a gruff voice through the intercom

"Can you take a package for Mr. Kinross, there doesn't appear to be anybody in?"

"No, I can't. I'm sick to death of taking bloody deliveries for other people."

The intercom went dead. Mike stormed back to the car, yanked the door open and hurled the box into the back seat, watching as it bounced off the other packages and landed on the floor. He got in, grinding his teeth, and shot off down the road.

The sun was high in the sky as Mike continued to drive. His stomach began to rumble, he glanced at the dashboard clock, 2pm, maybe just one more delivery and he could get something to eat. His phone bleeped.

Trevor: Haven't you finished yet?

Mike ignored it and gripped the steering wheel until his knuckles went white. He drove into a new housing estate and looked at all the large, detached houses with the sun radiating on their green lawns. It was a different world to his own small flat. He would love to stretch out on that lush grass and breathe in the clear air. He stopped outside a house with a shiny Mercedes Benz on the driveway. Once more he rummaged through the boxes before lifting a small, flat parcel. He walked up the path and rang the bell. No reply. He looked at the car, somebody must be in. He rang again, but again no reply. The package was small and seemed flexible. He bent it in two and shoved it through the letterbox. Another one down, he thought, as he made his way back to the car. Suddenly, he heard barking. He turned swiftly around as a large dog raced across the lawn towards him. The barks turned to growls and he could see the sharp teeth as it got nearer. He bolted for his car, yanking open the door as the beast grabbed the bottom of his trousers in its mouth. He tugged his leg free, hearing the rip as the door slammed shut. The dog's snarling head appeared in the window. Mike looked at its salivating mouth and jagged teeth. The dog dropped to the ground and trotted back around the side of the house. Mike looked down at his trousers, a long tear causing the bottom to flap open. His stomach rumbled more loudly and he could feel another headache coming on. He revved the engine, how he hated this job.

Mike turned into the drive thru burger joint, pulled up at the intercom and rolled down his window.

"Can I take your order, please?"

"A cheeseburger, fries and cola."

"Is that everything?"

"Yea."

He crept along the narrow lane and joined a queue of cars. He looked feverishly at the clock and the parcels still mounted on the seats. The car inched forward as another message appeared on his phone.

Trevor: Where are you now?

He clenched his jaw tight.

The car inched alongside the window.

"That will be £5, please."

Mike handed over a crumpled note and moved onto to the next window. He took the bag and pulled back out onto the road. He put the cup in the holder and opened the bag on his lap, reaching in and scooping up a handful of chips and cramming them into his mouth as he drove.

Trevor: You are behind schedule.

148

Mike crunched the chips hard as he increased his speed, ripping the paper around the burger and snatching it out. As he squeezed it aggressively and bit into it sauce squirted from the bottom onto his torn trousers. He groaned and wiped his trousers with his fingers creating a visible red stain. He gritted his teeth hard and forced his foot down on the accelerator.

Trevor: If you do not complete your round do not bother coming in tomorrow.

Up ahead the traffic light changed from green to amber. Mike rammed the gear stick into third and pressed the accelerator. The engine screamed as the car increased speed. The light changed to red, Mike hammered the accelerator into the floor. The car shot through the red light just as a lorry moved out from the side road. The vehicles impacted with a deafening crash. Mike's car spun violently around before coming to rest, black smoke bellowing from the engine. His door was completely crushed in. Inside Mike remained motionless, his head slumped on his chest and blood seeping from his forehead.

Trevor sat at his desk, the local newspaper open in front of him, the headline on a side column reading, MAN KILLED IN ORCHARD ROAD INCIDENT. He looked through the window as a silver Jaguar pulled up, A tall man in a navy suit got out of the car and walked purposefully towards the building. Trevor leapt to his feet, straightening his tie as he sped out of the office.

"Derek! I did not expect you today."

Derek examined the rows of boxes.

"They will all be gone by the end of the day," said Trevor hurriedly.

The men went into the office, Derek moving behind the desk and sitting in Trevor's chair. He looked at the newspaper headline.

"This is a terrible business, very bad publicity for us."

Trevor remained silent

"I've been told he went through a red light?"

"So, it seems."

"You will need to recruit more drivers. Make sure you vet their accident record, we don't want a repeat of yesterday's incident."

"I'll get right on it," replied Trevor.

"Who was the dead man?"

"Mike Williams."

"Were the packages delivered/"

"I did it myself personally, well, those that were not damaged."

"Get more drivers or you will be doing that permanently."

It was dark as Trevor left the warehouse. He got into his car, yawned and turned on the engine. Beside him his phone bleeped. He picked it up and looked at the message.

"One last job."

Who was still delivering at this time of night, Trevor was certain everyone had finished for the day. He looked at the name, Mike.

Trevor woke up, bleary eyed, he had spent a sleepless night tossing and turning, the message going round and round in his mind. He lay on his back and stared at the ceiling, how had it appeared on his phone? Perhaps the phone had been damaged in the crash causing the transmission to be delayed. Yes, that is what it must have been. He got up feeling clearer in his thoughts and went into the shower.

An hour later he was back in his office and set to work with the recruitment of new drivers. Turnover was high, it did not take people long to realise the gig economy was not all it was cracked up to be: no holiday or sick pay, paying your own insurance, and car repairs, not to mention the rising costs of paying for fuel. People were being sold that in the gig economy you could be your own boss, work your own hours and make big money into the bargain, it was nothing more than the modern version of the Emperor's New Clothes. His phone bleeped, another message.

"One last job."

The same text, Mike. He stared at it and felt a chill go down his spine. Mike was dead, he knew it, another faulty transmission caused by the crash. or was someone playing games with him? Surely the police would have all the contents from the accident. Unless they had been given to a family member. He put the phone face down and tried to concentrate on his work.

151

A few days later and the driver situation was getting bad, he even had to make some more deliveries himself at the end of the day. With the last delivery made he made his way home in the darkness. His phone bleeped, he looked wearily at the screen.

"One last job."

He slammed on the brakes, screeching to an abrupt halt. This could not go on. He clicked on Mike and pressed ring. A constant tone emitted from the phone, the line was dead. He threw the phone down, whipped the steering wheel around violently and did a U-turn in the road, the tyres squealing on the tarmac as he raced back into town.

The police station was empty. He walked uncertainly up to the desk and pressed the buzzer. All was quiet as he looked around the reception area. He pressed the buzzer again. A door at the back opened and a young officer appeared.

"Yes, sir?"

"Ah, yes, I'm looking for some information. There was a crash on the Orchard Road a few days ago, a man was killed, Mike Williams."

The officer nodded in acknowledgement.

"He has something of mine and I wondered who would have his belongings from the car?"

"They are here. Are you a relation of the deceased?"

"No, a work colleague."

"The belongings will be given to his next of kin."

"I only want to look at something."

"I'm sorry, sir, that is not permissible."

Trevor removed his wallet and put a £50 note on the desk.

"Are you trying to bribe a police officer?"

Trevor put a second £50 beside it.

"I just want to look at his phone."

The officer looked at the notes. He grabbed them quickly and shoved them in his pocket before disappearing back through the door.

Trevor paced up and down.

The officer returned with a small box. Trevor looked inside: keys, wallet, phone. He picked it up.

"We had it unlocked to check," said the officer.

Trevor switched the phone on and went to messages. He clicked on the conversation line between himself and Mike and read the last message.

Trevor: If you do not complete your round do not bother coming in tomorrow.

He recognised it as the last message he had sent just prior to the crash. After that the screen was blank, the "one last job" messages were gone.

"Has anyone used this phone?" he asked desperately.

"This is just how it was found."

He placed the phone back in the box and walked slowly away in a daze.

Trevor was at work early the next day. There were stacks of boxes and fewer and fewer drivers. Who could blame them, it was a grim job. He looked at the morning paper as he drank his tea. Flicking through the pages lazily he stopped at births, deaths and marriages. He scanned down the list of deaths and read the last entry; *Mike Williams, funeral today at St. David's Church, 3pm.* He sipped his tea and reclined back in his chair. Why were there no texts on Mike's phone, "one last job?" Another glitch? He cupped the mug feeling the heat warm his hands. Outside he heard a lorry pulling up, a new delivery to add to the mountain he groaned, putting down the mug and heading out.

****

Trevor collapsed back in his chair and glanced at his watch, 2.45pm and he had not even had lunch. He opened a small plastic box and took out a ham sandwich biting ravenously into it. His phone bleeped.

"One last job."

He dropped the sandwich and seized the newspaper. The funeral was at 3pm. He grabbed his coat and stumbled through the door in his haste, getting into his car and speeding down the road.

By the time he got to the graveyard it was 4pm, the service was over and he found the graveyard deserted. He moved from grave to grave scanning the epitaphs on the headstones until he found the one he was looking for, MIKE WILLIAMS. There were no flowers, just a small grey headstone. Suddenly, he became aware of something gliding between the trees surrounding the cemetery. It stopped as he focused on it. Its shape was human yet it seemed to shimmer in a white hue. The blood froze in Trevor's veins, he was statuesque, transfixed by the apparition. The word "Mike" slipped quietly from his lips. He moved slowly towards it. The vision stayed still. Trevor could feel his heart beating faster and his breathing fast and heavy. He moved closer and closer, the figure not flinching. Trevor increased his pace.

"Mike?" he called breaking into a run.

Suddenly he stumbled falling to his knees on the wet grass. He ambled to his feet and looked up, the apparition was gone.

"Where have you been?" demanded Derek as Trevor returned to the office.

"I just had to check something,"

"I'll tell you what to check, the amount of packages to be delivered."

Trevor looked at the never ending pile of boxes.

"Get the job done, I don't care if you have to deliver them yourself."

It was dark outside and rain was beginning to fall as Trevor looked at the deserted yard and the dozen boxes still remaining. He loaded up his car and set off. The sky was dark and rain was beginning to fall, Trevor drove from house to house dropping off the boxes until only one remained. He placed it on the seat beside him and looked at the label. His face turned white as he read the name, Mike Williams.

The rain was getting heavier as Trevor stopped and looked up at the grey apartment block. He pulled the zip of his jacket up to the top and turned up the collar, picked up the package and opened the door. The rain pounded down on him as he moved quickly to the entrance. The electronic lock was broken, he pulled back the door and he went inside. The foyer was gloomy, a dim single light illuminating the flaking grey paint. He looked at the out of order sign on the lift and started climbing the stairs. Thoughts were racing through his mind: the constant messages, the package, the figure in the graveyard.. He arrived on the sixth floor and moved slowly along the corridor. Stopping in front of the door at the end and read the name plate "Mike Williams." He knocked on the door. As his fist hit the wood it eased open. He peered through the crack into the darkness. Pushing it further open, he was immediately hit with an acrid stench causing him to cover his nose and mouth and the icy cold air. He entered the apartment and pressed the light switch. The hall remained dark. He pressed it again toggling it up and down feverishly. Placing the package on the floor and proceeded cautiously into the sitting room, feeling the cold chill his body, so much that he could see the breath in front of his face. The uncovered window emitted enough light to make out the outline of the sofa and table. Suddenly the door slammed behind him. He turned quickly around.

156

"Who's there?" he blurted, feeling his heart beat faster.

The curtains swayed gently. He moved forwards until he was in reach of the curtains. They moved lightly. Trevor steeled himself, lifted his hand and gently gripped the edge of the material. Quickly he whipped the curtain back. He heard the hiss and saw the burning green eyes causing him to recoil and fall backwards onto the sofa. The cat jumped from the window sill onto the carpet. Trevor wiped the perspiration from his forehead and let out a huge sigh of relief. The cat looked at him, In his pocket he heard a bleep. Tentatively he reached inside and removed the phone. The icon displayed one message. His hand began to shake as he moved his finger over the icon and pressed.

"One last job."

He looked at the screen, his eyes wild with terror. The cat arched his back and hissed, exposing its sharp teeth. Trevor bolted to the door, grabbing the handle and turning it, The door remained firmly closed. He rattled the handle up and down and tugged violently but it refused to open. The phone bleeped again. He banged furiously on the door, his knuckles began to bleed. The phone bleeped again and again. He started ramming the door with his shoulder. The frame shuddered with each hit but still the phone bleeped. He yanked it from his pocket, the screen was filled with messages.

"One last job."

"One last job."

"One last job."

"One last job."

He hurled the phone to the floor and looked desperately around the room. Through the window he could see the fire escape stairwell. He lurched across the room and tugged open the balcony door, staggering out and towards the stairs. He felt the rain falling on him, he did not care, he was out. All he wanted to do was get home to safety. He raced to the stairwell and started to descend, his foot caught in the hole propelling him head first over the banister. His scream rang out until he hit the hard, concrete ground. Blood seeped out from the back of his skull as his body remained motionless. In the flat above his phone bleeped for the final time.

"Job complete."

A J BOOTHMAN

OTHER BOOKS

TWIST IN THE TALE SHORT STORIES VOLUME 1

Spellbinding short stories of intrigue and suspense with dramatic and unexpected endings.

The Attic

Sheeba

Vampire

A Dark Winter's Tale

Swipe Right

Stranger in The Night

Snake

Ice

The Last Train

Trench Warfare

THE RAVEN'S VENGEANCE

The first Teagan O'Riordan mystery.

Events from the past spawn great vengeance in the sleepy Irish village of Rathkilleen. To catch a killer Detective Teagan O'Riordan will have to discover the secret of the Raven.

A complex mystery thriller that embraces Irish culture and reaches across Africa.

TEAGAN AND THE ANGEL OF DEATH

The second Teagan O'Riordan mystery.

Devil worshippers bring sacrilege and death to Rathkilleen. Teagan has to unravel satanic rituals and demonic symbols in order to unmask the Angel of Death.

An intricate mystery thriller which extends across Europe.

SHEER HATE

The Vigil is a vicious online newspaper that revels in muckraking and delights in ruining lives, leaving a trail of victims in its wake with deadly consequences. Seductive reporter, Silky Stevens, and sleazy photographer, Frank Ebdon, will do anything to get a front-page story. Journalist, Nick Rose, struggles with his past, but is forced to use all his investigative skills to unmask a killer driven by sheer hate.

THE RIPPER CLUB

A grisly murder sets computer hacker, Chris, and psychology student, Emma, on the trail of a serial killer and the discovery of the mysterious Ripper Club. Their investigations take them back to Whitechapel 1888 and Jack the Ripper. As the story unfolds and the suspense builds, the connections between the past and the present are revealed. Can they identify the killer before it is too late?

JACKPOT MILLIONAIRE

Danny Taylor is a middle-aged, working-class bloke who dreams of a better life away from the drudgery of work and his mundane, repetitive existence. He fantasises about being rich and having fast cars and even faster women. All this could become a reality if only he could win the lottery. Would this really lead to the fantastic life he imagines?

Jackpot Millionaire is a hilarious, fast paced comedy.

Printed in Great Britain
by Amazon